Dear Reader,

Welcome back to Buckhorn!

Though I know an actual Buckhorn exists, mine is an entirely fictional town in beautiful Kentucky. My first Buckhorn story was published back in 2000 and the series has become a true reader favorite. For me it seemed a natural fit to combine my need to help stray cats and dogs with continuing the series about a new generation of the leading family in Buckhorn.

Through a special contract with my publisher, the advance and all royalties on this story will go directly to the Animal Adoption Foundation, a local no-kill animal shelter that does an amazing job healing, protecting and loving cats and dogs until a "forever home" can be found for them.

I hope you enjoy the story, and I especially hope you enjoy knowing that by purchasing this story, you've helped a dog or cat in need.

To see other "benefit books," visit lorifoster.com/benefit-books.

And to see other books in the Buckhorn series, visit lorifoster.com/connected-books/#buckhorn.

From the bottom of my heart, thank you!

*Lori Foster*

**Lori Foster** is a *New York Times*, *USA TODAY* and *Publishers Weekly* bestselling author with books from a variety of publishers, including Berkley/Jove, Kensington, St. Martin's, Harlequin and Silhouette. Lori has been a recipient of the prestigious *RT Book Reviews* Career Achievement Award for Series Romantic Fantasy and for Contemporary Romance. For more about Lori, visit her website at www.lorifoster.com.

# LORI FOSTER
# A BUCKHORN
## BACHELOR

*Alexandria,*
*Happy reading!*
*Lori Foster*

**HQN**™

If you purchased this book without a cover you should be aware that this book is stolen property. It was reported as "unsold and destroyed" to the publisher, and neither the author nor the publisher has received any payment for this "stripped book."

**HQN**™

ISBN-13: 978-1-460-39766-4

A Buckhorn Bachelor & A Buckhorn Summer

Copyright © 2016 by Lori Foster

The publisher acknowledges the copyright holder of the individual works as follows:

A Buckhorn Bachelor
Copyright © 2016 by Lori Foster

A Buckhorn Summer
Copyright © 2015 by Lori Foster

All rights reserved. Except for use in any review, the reproduction or utilization of this work in whole or in part in any form by any electronic, mechanical or other means, now known or hereinafter invented, including xerography, photocopying and recording, or in any information storage or retrieval system, is forbidden without the written permission of the publisher, HQN Books, 225 Duncan Mill Road, Don Mills, Ontario M3B 3K9, Canada.

This is a work of fiction. Names, characters, places and incidents are either the product of the author's imagination or are used fictitiously, and any resemblance to actual persons, living or dead, business establishments, events or locales is entirely coincidental.

This edition published by arrangement with Harlequin Books S.A.

For questions and comments about the quality of this book, please contact us at CustomerService@Harlequin.com.

® and ™ are trademarks of Harlequin Enterprises Limited or its corporate affiliates. Trademarks indicated with ® are registered in the United States Patent and Trademark Office, the Canadian Intellectual Property Office and in other countries.

www.HQNBooks.com

**Printed in U.S.A.**

Recycling programs for this product may not exist in your area.

# CONTENTS

A BUCKHORN BACHELOR — 7

A BUCKHORN SUMMER — 111

To the Animal Adoption Foundation,
www.AAFPets.org

Thank you for all you do to help dogs and cats in need. I know my contributions are always put to very good use. It's been a true pleasure watching the AAF grow!

# A BUCKHORN
## —BACHELOR—

## *CHAPTER ONE*

ADAM SOMMERVILLE STROLLED around the perimeter of the carnival, keeping watch on the kids and checking out the different games and rides while also steering clear of the clingier ladies. Being an almost-thirty-year-old bachelor from a leading family in a small town made him prime pickings. Even in the fun atmosphere of the carnival, the sunny June weather, and the crowds who'd turned out to support the elementary school, he wasn't safe from marriage-minded ladies. Especially when members of his own family conspired against him. Many of them figured it was past time for him to settle down.

How the hell had he gotten so old?

Thirty. The big three-oh.

He didn't feel thirty, yet. For sure he wasn't ready for it. Not that he obsessed on age or anything. He had a terrific life, a life he loved. He enjoyed being free and clear, taking on only those responsibilities of his choosing.

Like his insane, enormous, and awesome family.

Or his job as an elementary school gym teacher, which suited him perfectly.

But he had to admit, lately it felt like something was missing.

Maybe because he'd never planned to stay…alone.

Snorting at himself, Adam kept walking, trying to out-pace his thoughts. He wasn't *alone*, not in that maudlin, depressed way. He had a wealth of relatives, plenty of good friends, and whenever he needed it, he found female companionship.

Tonight seemed like one of those nights.

The oppressive heat added to his edginess. The thrumming carnival music and laughter from kids made him think of things he didn't have, things he hadn't even thought about wanting.

Damn.

*He definitely needed to get laid.*

Wearing reflective sunglasses worked in Adam's favor. He could scope out prospective company for later without anyone knowing, dodge left or right to avoid engaging women who always crowded his space, and he could ignore particular ladies—like Cindy, who'd just turned twenty—who he knew would only be trouble.

Just as turning thirty shocked him, so too did the idea of a female being too damn young. But there it was, the bald truth.

He was getting older and although he felt like a traitor to bachelors everywhere, he knew he needed more than giggling enthusiasm, a hot body, and blind agreement.

Pausing beneath the shade of a tall tree, Adam looked around at the colorful movement of summer T-shirts. So many women, yet thanks to this new weird awareness he had of his internal clock ticking away, he didn't feel a single prickle of interest.

He could blame his cousin for that. She was the one who'd started the nagging about him being a bachelor.

And once Amber had started, the others had chimed in and—

"Yer daddy wasn't a glassmaker."

Surprised, Adam looked behind him and saw Isabella Presley, the petite middle school librarian, seated on a quilt. She had her dark red hair in a high ponytail, her arms braced behind her and her legs stretched out with her sedate summer dress tucked in around her slim thighs. She'd taken off her shoes and for some insane reason, Adam zeroed in on her small naked feet.

She had painted her toenails fire engine red. Her feet looked soft, finely arched—

"Now see," she said in her southern-Kentucky accent, "that was a hint that I'd like you to move. Your daddy not being a glassmaker means I can't see through you."

Isabella hadn't been born in Buckhorn, Kentucky. No, she'd moved "up north" five years ago, yet retained her heavier drawl and an appealing accent. When she said "can't," it sounded like "cain't" and always made him smile.

"I got it." Pulling off his sunglasses, Adam moved to the side of her. "Mind if I join you?"

For an answer, she scooted over. Gazing out at the carnival crowd now that he didn't block her view, she said, "Take a load off."

"Thanks." Copying her, Adam removed his sneakers and lowered himself beside her. Their arms brushed. The slightest of breezes brought the sweet fragrance of her sun-warmed skin to his nose. Every part of his body noticed.

Trying to ignore the sudden awareness zinging

through his blood, he asked casually, "You supervising, too?"

"Nope. Just enjoyin'." When the breeze picked up, parting the leaves of the overhead branches and letting in the blistering sunshine, Isabella wrinkled her nose and squinted her blue eyes. "Sure is hot today."

Adam peeled his damp T-shirt away from his chest and nodded agreement. Heat and humidity left his khaki shorts limp. More than his shirt was sticking. "Low nineties."

"Swelterin'."

"Typical for this time of year."

"Mm-hmm." Suddenly she grinned.

"What?"

Lifting one lightly freckled shoulder, she said, "Just struck me funny, that's all."

Not following, he looked at her face, and smiled at the amusement there. "What did?"

"*Me* shootin' the breeze with *you*." She leaned a little closer until her shoulder deliberately bumped his again. "Buckhorn's most wanted bachelor, pausin' from his prowl to visit with little ole me. Ya gotta admit, it's amusin'."

With her tilted toward him that way, her face turned up to his, Adam suddenly thought about kissing. Hot, tongue-twining, consuming kissing.

With her.

*Damn*.

Since he'd known Isabella, he'd never once thought about getting his mouth on her.

At least, not seriously.

From the day she'd moved to his town, they'd been friendly, sometimes working together on school fundraisers or serving together on committees. Sure, he always enjoyed her company, but the fact that they saw each other within their careers at the school made anything more than friendship dicey.

Or at least that's how he usually figured it.

Now...not so much. "Issy," he teased back. "You flirting with me?"

Instead of denying it, as he expected, she lowered her lashes and gave a lazy shrug. "Honin' my skills for later, ya know?"

What the hell did that mean? "No," he said, trying to wade carefully. "I don't know."

"You're a big fibber, Adam Sommerville. You know in a few hours when the sun sets and the stars come out, you'll be findin' yourself some company. The glasses didn't fool me. You were scopin' out the prospects."

Had he really been so obvious? Rather than deny it, he asked the obvious question. "What does that have to do with you?"

Wearing the slightest of devilish smiles, she stared out at the crowds. "I'll probably be doin' the same, that's all. I figure by ten at the latest, the guys left will be the available ones who'd be interested. So I might try my hand at the pick-up game."

*The pick-up game.*

Why the hell did that annoy him so much? He wasn't her keeper, he had no claim on her, and...to heck with it.

Adam yanked off the sunglasses and frowned at her. "If that's your plan, why are you flirting with me?"

Indolent, and somehow sexier because of it, she sighed. "You weren't listenin'? Already told you I was honing my skills." She wrinkled her small nose. "Bein' a librarian means I know a lil bit about a lot, but pickin' up company isn't in my repertoire. Knowin' you aren't interested makes you safe for…" She looked up at him and smiled. "Practice."

Of all the… Feeling strangely annoyed, Adam stretched out to his back and folded an arm over his eyes. "You're nuts, Issy."

"Celibacy can do that to a woman."

From his eyebrows to his toes, Adam stilled. Plunged into curiosity, he lifted his arm away and stared at her. "Celibacy?"

She gave a self-deprecating grin. "It's been a mighty long time, that's all I'm sayin'."

He searched her face, a face he knew well, and saw no signs of teasing. She meant what she said.

Isabella, librarian extraordinaire, planned to get laid. Tonight. With some bozo from the carnival.

*How long had she been without?*

Adam thought back over the time he'd known her. Isabella had dated a few times, but he couldn't recall her being in any serious relationship. She stayed super-involved in the school, hyper-serious about kids reading, and she put in plenty of free time assisting disadvantaged kids and those with learning disabilities.

She stayed active, with work, charity, kids.

Just not with men.

So many times he'd wondered why she wasn't married with a few kids of her own. Anyone who knew her also knew she'd be an amazing mother. Smart, dedicated, friendly, caring…and now that he allowed himself to dwell on it, he had to admit she was cute.

Or maybe more like smokin'—in a seriously sweet and approachable way. It was her accent and teasing wit that made "cute" come to mind. That, and her understated wardrobe...fit for a librarian.

He reminded himself that her proximity at work remained an issue. Only at the moment, sitting here with her in the hot sunshine, breathing in her scent, that didn't seem to matter much.

To be honest, he could admit the friend vibe had originated with her. From day one, she'd relegated him to "work pal" status, without ever really giving him a chance to decide if he wanted to go for more.

And now that he thought about it, that sort of burned his ass a little. He wasn't a masochist and wasn't into chasing disinterested women, not when there were enough of the other kind to keep him busy. So then why-"You do seem to wander off inside your own head, don't ya?" To take the sting out of that criticism, Isabella half smiled.

But it stung all the same. "I was just thinking."

"No, Sugar, you were daydreamin'." She lazily fanned her face and throat. "There's a difference."

Sugar? Adam knew she often addressed the kids that way. And when looking for new funding for her much-loved library, everyone was her "Sugar." But him?

First time.

She could easily charm students, parents, and the school board alike. But before now, she'd never openly attempted to charm him.

Suddenly the idea of a casual hookup with some other woman didn't interest him. Nope.

Adam wanted to seduce Ms. Issy.

Once decided, he didn't question himself. Why bother? The thought of having her was far more exciting than anything else had been in months. He felt more alive, and the sweltering summer heat had nothing on his rising internal temp.

His gaze tracked over her face to her throat, now looking dewy. "You want my help?" The second he made the offer, his heart started thumping hard.

He ignored it. This had nothing to do with his heart.

She took him off guard by stretching out next to him on her side, her head propped on a fist as she studied him. "Interestin'," she mused. "How exactly would you assist?"

Damn, when Isabella decided to flirt, she excelled. He should have expected that because everything she did, she did with perfection. It wasn't what she said, but how she said it.

How she *looked* while saying it. Sort of interested and amused and a little turned on.

Crowds milled past them only a few feet away. He felt the curious stares, heard the whispers.

And flat-out didn't care.

Visually tracing the curvy line of her body, he took in the shape of her slim thighs, the rise of her hip and contrasting dip of her waist, up to her creamy bare shoulders exposed by the narrow straps of her sundress.

Freckles had never looked more enticing.

"You have on sunscreen?" Even here in the cool, lush grass with the elm leaves shading them, she could easily burn.

After a priceless look, Issy blinked, then dropped to her back laughing. Not a loud or harsh laugh, but not a ridiculous twitter either. She sounded husky and sincere.

Enjoying her, Adam loomed over her. "You expected something more intimate from me?"

Eyes twinkling, she whispered with a smile, "Silly me."

How had he missed the length and thickness of her dark brown lashes, or the faint sprinkling of freckles over the bridge of her nose, or how her mouth, always free of lipstick, looked so full and soft? "Maybe I should explain the path of my thoughts."

"The path that led to sunscreen? Oh, I can't wait to hear it."

The ever-stirring breeze carried a baby soft tendril of fiery hair across her face. Without giving it enough thought, Adam used one fingertip to brush it back, tucking it behind her small ear.

Isabella's gaze smoldered.

From such a simple touch? And if so, how would she be when he had her naked and touched her all over? He gave a low growl that she answered with fast blinking, as if coming out of a spell.

Breathless, she asked, "What was that?"

He knew what she meant, of course, but said only, "What?"

"That macho sound you made." No hesitation from Isabella.

As if unsure, he suggested, "Reaction?"

Excited by the prospect, she came up to her elbow again. "You *growled* at me."

"I growled at my unruly imagination."

Her eyebrow lifted. She glanced at his mouth then back to his eyes, and breathed, "Tell me."

Tell her that he'd visualized her naked, in bed—with him?

Not a great idea. Yet. Shoot, they'd only just started the whole flirting business.

Twirling one finger, Adam took the safer route. "Let's rewind to my thoughts."

She made a face. "You gonna ask me about my last dental appointment?"

Damn, but she confused him.

"You know, since staring down at me made you wonder about sunscreen?" She flapped a hand. "There's no tellin' what you're thinkin' now."

He trailed a finger over her silky shoulder, across to her collarbone, then up to lift her stubborn chin so those pretty blue eyes focused on him. "I was thinking about this soft, pale skin of yours. How fair and delicate you are. That's what made me worry about the sun."

Dubious, she shifted her gaze to her own shoulder, rolled it, and said, "I don't know about delicate, but I do burn easily. So yes to the sunscreen. And now… about that wicked imagination of yours?"

A shadow fell across them and Adam looked up to see his cousin, Amber, staring down at them. Hands on her hips, a frown on her face, she chastised him with nothing more than a look of extreme disappointment.

Knowing he was caught, Adam sat up, winced at the new tightness in his shorts, and dropped his elbows to his knees. "What's up, Amber?"

"You're causing a spectacle."

Issy, too, sat up. "We are?"

"*He* is."

"I'm with him." She gave a slow smile. "And honestly, Amber, I sort of like the idea of bein' a spectacle for once."

## *CHAPTER TWO*

ADAM PACED IN front of the grill where fresh corn on the cob filled the air with mouth-watering scents. People lined up twenty deep, waiting to buy an ear. His cousins Shohn and Garrett ran the grill, but in five minutes he'd take over for Shohn.

*Where was Isabella?*

He'd had to leave her alone with Amber, and God knew no good would come from that. He adored Amber, everyone did, but the girl did like to meddle. Big time. And she'd looked disapproving, so heaven only knew where her unwelcome meddling would lead this time.

Naturally he knew why she'd been disapproving. Amber had a favorite, very insulting narrative she used to describe his preference for variety.

*"You skate through women like it's a sport."*

How many times had she given him that complaint? Usually he laughed at her.

He didn't feel like laughing this time.

Would she encourage Isabella to find a different guy? One more settled? A man who'd be better relationship material?

If Issy even wanted that.

Picking up a leftover guy at a town carnival didn't sound like anything serious to him. But he'd never gotten the impression that Issy was the "fast and easy" type, either. Everything about her screamed "nice girl," the type you brought home to meet your mom.

Adam knew *his* mom would love her.

He shouldn't care about Issy's plans, but he'd already worked himself up about it and—

Shohn shoved an apron at him. "Your turn."

Drawn from his thoughts, Adam eyed the utilitarian apron and shoved it back at Shohn. "I'm ready."

Shohn looked him over, caught his arm, and dragged him a few feet away to say, "I heard you were making out with Isabella Presley right in front of God and sundry."

*What the hell?*

"We weren't *making out*." He scoffed. "We were talking."

"Horizontal talking? With you stroking her face?"

Snatching the apron back, Adam tied it on just to give himself something to do other than look guilty. "Horizontal, yes." As Shohn's eyes widened, Adam clarified, "On a picnic quilt, resting in the shade. But I wasn't *stroking* her." He'd wanted to. All over. With hands and lips...

But he'd managed to refrain that much.

"We were talking, period." About getting laid.

Or maybe it was laying each other.

Issy had put him into such a blind tailspin, he couldn't even remember everything he'd said.

"All right, don't blow a gasket. I just wondered." Shohn smiled at an elderly couple who strolled past, then laughed at two grade school boys who flew by with blue cotton candy faces and excitement in their eyes. "If I hadn't heard about her shaking off the old-maid mantle, I might not have thought anything of it. But word has it that Isabella is looking to take a turn on the wild side."

Adam stared at him, horrified, suspicious, and damn it, a little jealous. "What are you talking about?"

"Rumors, that's all." Shohn whacked him on the shoulder. "Don't give it another thought."

Like he'd be able to think about anything else now? "Where'd you hear these so-called rumors?"

"From Amber."

Well, that explained nothing. Everyone knew Amber had very odd ideas about things—and often saw what others didn't.

His thoughts churning, Adam watched Shohn walk away.

"Hey, a little help here?"

He turned to see Garrett overwhelmed with a hungry horde looking for corn. "Right, sorry." With the apron in place, he stepped in and for the next half hour they served over a hundred ears of corn. Finally, once the band started playing from the stage at the other end of the lot, the crowd headed in a new direction.

"Wow." After dousing his face in icy water from the cooler, Garrett used a hand towel to dry off. "Between the heat of the grill and that broiling sun, I'm feeling as roasted as the corn."

"Yeah." Distracted, Adam fished out a chunk of ice and used it on the back of his neck. It helped a little, but with his imagination again on Isabella, what she might be doing—and who she might plan on doing it with—he was still too hot.

"May I?"

At the sound of that twangy voice, he jerked around

and there she was, smiling at him. The evening sun gilded her gorgeous hair, highlighting the red and showing the richness of it. Her eyes were so very blue, her pale skin flushed. Between her breasts, her dress was slightly damp.

Adam felt himself reacting and didn't understand it. *What was it about her?* Besides her hotness. And teasing. And sweet little body...

She turned to Garrett. "He does this often, sort of goes off in his own head. Has your family ever had him tested?"

Amusement thick in his tone, Garrett said, "I don't think so, but I can make the recommendation."

"Might be a good idea." She looked at Adam again, tilted her head, then held out a hand. "The ice?"

He got it together and fetched her a fresh chunk. Anxious to see what she'd do, he stepped to the edge of the booth and braced his hands on the top beside the butter and salt.

Right there, in front of everyone—which mostly was just him and Garrett—she tipped her head back and rolled that ice over her throat and upper chest.

*Lord have mercy.*

"It is so hot." Lifting her ponytail, she tipped her head forward and teased the ice down her nape. A droplet trailed along her slender throat, over her shoulder and onto her chest. "Oh, that's better. Nice."

Adam swallowed.

After an elbow to the ribs and a sly grin, Garrett said, "I think I'll take a break. Man the fort, okay?"

"Yeah. Sure. Whatever." He peeled off his apron and stepped out of the booth to close in on Issy. "What do you think you're doing?"

"Coolin' down."

While heating him up. "You look like you're making a porno."

Her eyes flared...with delight. "I do?" She flashed her glance around but now that Garrett had booked, no one was close. "I was...sexy? Seriously?"

How the hell could she not know that? "You're getting me hard."

She started to look down.

Adam put his fingers under her chin, keeping her gaze on his face. If she looked, there'd be no "getting" to it. He'd have a full-fledged boner. "What's more, I think you know it."

"I didn't, but thank you for tellin' me." She licked her lips. "I've been tryin' to watch other ladies, to see how they flirt. Your cousin gave me some pointers."

He dropped his hand, blinked, drew a breath—and had to ask. "Amber?"

"Yes. She knows somethin' about everythin', doesn't she?"

"Sure thinks she does." Scowling, Adam looked around but didn't see Amber anywhere. He zeroed back in on Issy. "It's not a great idea to take advice from her."

"Then from whom should I take it?" She stepped closer, tipping her head back to keep eye contact. "You?"

The breeze was long gone, but as the sun faded behind the hills the heat lost its edge, making the evening air feel more tolerable. Still hot, but not so smothering. Around them, the carnival lights flickered on.

Feeling like they were talking about things other than advice, Adam said, "I offered, remember?"

"I remember that you failed to specify exactly what you were offerin'."

*Anything you want.* But maybe he should stop being so eager. Maybe he'd do better to tease back a little. Going with that plan, he said, "You could start by practicing your flirting skills on me."

"Oh, I *love* that idea." Smiling, she slowly touched his chest, stroked with her fingertips, lowered her lashes, and asked, "How's that?"

Hell, he felt that light touch clear down to his shorts. After clearing his throat, he said, "Effective." *He sounded like a strangling frog.*

"So if I seek out other guys tonight…" She walked her fingers back up his chest to his shoulder. "…you think I'd be successful?"

"At *what?*"

"I'm lonely," she complained with a sexy pout, her fingers still on the move, now teasing the damp ends of hair over his nape. "I need company, no matter how temporary."

Suspicious, unaccountably irate, Adam clarified, "Company, meaning sex?"

She smiled in a very provocative way. "That'd depend on the guy and how things progressed."

*Not happening.* Adam claimed her hand with his, brought it down to his chest and flattened her palm over his heart. "How about you slow your roll on that?"

Ferris wheel lights glittered in her eyes.

Or maybe that was a pissed-off glitter. Hard to know.

"So tell me, Sugar, you plannin' to *slow your roll* tonight?"

"If I'm with you, sure." *What the hell was he saying?*

"Instead of you running off to sleep with some nameless—" *and lucky*

"—dude, how about we enjoy the carnival? You can keep flirting. I'll tell you what works." Which so far had been everything. "And in the meantime we could have some fun." Not the type of fun he'd really like to have, but at the moment, he enjoyed her company enough that he could make a concession.

"Hmm."

Watching her take her own sweet time thinking about his offer bugged Adam big time. It should've been an easy decision. By now, other women would have said-"Okay."

He released a tense breath.

"On one condition."

His teeth locked and he cocked a brow in query.

Looking very stern and determined, she said, "End of the night, no matter how things go otherwise, I at least get a kiss."

Whoa. After the craziness of this current interaction with her, Adam refused to make assumptions. "From who?"

"Why, from *you*, silly."

He forgot they were in the open, that kids and their parents milled around them. Neighbors and teachers. The principal. Members of the school board.

His own meddling family.

All he could think about was getting his mouth on hers.

Catching her narrow waist in his hands, Adam slowly drew her in. "If it's to be guaranteed, why save it for the end of the night? We could just start right off with—"

"There you are." Amber swooped in with Noel Poet in tow. Far too enthusiastically, she pulled Issy away and locked her to her side. "I've been looking all over for you, Isabella. Noel has some men for you to meet."

*What the hell?* Adam narrowed his eyes on Noel.

Noel immediately held up his hands. "Not my doing."

"Don't be modest," Amber said, flipping her long dark braid. "Noel easily racked up three guys, all of them perfect."

Damn it, he'd been about to kiss her. The last thing he wanted was for Amber to whisk her off to some other guy.

With biting irritation, Adam asked, "Perfect for *what?*"

At almost the same time, Issy said, "Really? For me?"

"Uh..." Noel looked like he wanted to make a run for it—until Amber took his hand. Then the putz melted.

It seemed to Adam that Amber and Noel made a most unlikely pair. But whether they admitted or not, that's what they seemed to be—sort of.

As a firefighter, Noel worked with Amber's brother, Garrett, which was where Amber had met him. Since then they'd been dancing around each other, not really a declared couple, but at every big community function they ended up together.

Amber had long dark hair and blue eyes.

Noel was blond with brown eyes.

But the contrasts didn't end with their appearances. Where Noel seemed quietly contained and often far too serious, Amber was bold, incredibly outspoken and carefree.

Sure, she was pretty enough to reel in any guy, but he'd assumed Noel had enough backbone to keep from being drawn into her scheming.

When Amber only smiled, Adam grated, "What guys?"

Shaking his head, Noel said to Amber, "I think we're interrupting."

"Don't be silly."

Noel said evenly, "I am never silly."

Amber just smiled at him. "Isabella already asked for my recommendations, and I'm giving them." Her gaze raked over Adam. "And that's that."

Issy laughed. "Well, I don't suppose it'd hurt for me to take a little look, now would it?"

Of all the... Adam narrowed his eyes. "You can't be serious."

"I'll be right back," she promised, and patted his chest—like he was a damned wayward mutt.

Stunned, Adam stared down at her. He had no idea what to say, so he said nothing.

Issy waited, but with his extended silence her smile faltered, and finally she looked away. "Noel? Are you ready?"

Very ill at ease, Noel hitched his chin. "Sure."

"I'll join you in a minute," Amber told them.

Still disbelieving, Adam watched Issy walk away, her hand in the crook of Noel's elbow, until he couldn't see her anymore.

"So," Amber started.

"Forget it." Beyond peeved at her, Adam headed back into the booth. She'd already done enough. No way in hell would he listen to some half-baked lecture from her.

Of course she followed.

"She's all wrong for you, Adam."

He leveled a sharp look on her. "Contrary to what every wimp in the county tells you, you do not know everything."

It was never easy to put a dent in Amber's confidence. "I realize that. But I do know *you*. And I also know Isabella."

Folding his arms over his chest, his temper on the rise, Adam said, "So what? You think I'd break her heart or something?"

She gave a surprised laugh that she quickly muffled with a cough. "No, I wasn't concerned about that."

Adam waited her out, his scowl not budging.

After another cough, Amber got serious. "I hope you won't think I'm gossiping—"

"Shohn already told me what you said."

"I only told him so he could tell you in case I didn't get to you in time. Even before I'd reached you two, I knew you were playing with Issy. *Everyone* was talking about it."

"Define everyone."

"People who'd passed the two of you. Ms. Marburl was scandalized. Little Chuck started singing that you had a girlfriend. When I stopped at the corn booth, Shohn didn't know where you were but he said you were due to replace him at any minute. So I told him."

"Told him that Issy is a wild child?" He snorted. "That's nuts and you know it."

"Oh, Adam." With a pitying look, Amber patted his arm. "You've known her all this time and yet…you don't really know her at all."

## *CHAPTER THREE*

ISABELLA HAD A hard time keeping her smile in place as she walked away from Adam. She didn't want to meet any other men, and she definitely didn't plan to get intimate with anyone—well, except maybe Adam.

If he was still willing.

"You okay?" Noel asked.

"Course I am."

"You know, if you want, I can make your excuses to the guys. Say you got busy or something."

She peeked at him. "Is my disinterest that noticeable?"

"Afraid so." He paused with her under the lights of the roller coaster. They both looked up at the screaming riders as the coaster cars zipped by. "Amber has a tendency to bulldoze her way through life."

"She is confident." Sometimes Isabella envied Amber for her headstrong certainty.

"That's an understatement." Noel turned his speculative gaze down to her. "Don't let her bully you into doing anything you don't want to do."

Compelled to defend her friend, Isabella said, "She's actually been very helpful."

"And she always means well," Noel added. "I'll even admit that most of the time she knows what she's doing. But I've gotten to know her."

"Do tell."

One corner of his mouth curled. In a husky, satisfied-man voice he said, "Let's just stick to talking about you tonight."

Deflated, Isabella sighed. "If we must."

"Amber doesn't know men nearly as well as she thinks she does."

Oh, now that was interesting. "You came to this conclusion...how?"

"Because she's always playing games. And as a man—"

He was definitely all man.

"—I can tell you, we don't appreciate it."

"And yet," Isabella pointed out, "she's so often successful."

"How about we give a little credit to the men, too, okay? Yes, she hooked up Shohn with Nadine, and Garrett with Zoey, and Gray with Lisa-"

"You're ruinin' your own case."

Noel shook his head. "Making the point that while Amber might've pointed them in the right direction, or given a helping hand, she didn't make them fall in love. Each of the guys was smart enough to do that all on his own."

She peeked up at him. "That's what you think I want? To fall in love?"

After a commiserating smile, Noel took her arm and got her walking again. "I think you're already in love. What you want is for Adam to love you in return."

That insight so surprised her, she faltered a step.

How was it Noel knew that when no one else did? For sure Adam didn't suspect. If he did, he probably wouldn't be chatting with her now. She'd done her best to hide it, but she'd known for some time that he was the one for her.

It was party his great rapport with kids and his awesome contributions to the community . Adam was a very admirable man.

But it was also the way he carried himself, with pride and dignity, the way he pitched in to help others, the easy way he smiled.

Those dark bedroom eyes… She shivered, and admitted to herself that his body was pretty darned fine too.

But it was mostly his character, she assured herself. Sure he was great to look at, but she wouldn't love a man for his looks alone.

Realizing she'd gone too quiet, too long, Isabella stammered, "I, um… Why would you say such a thing?"

Noel stopped, faced her. "I saw you with him, and I'm not a dummy, either. Amber can play all the games she wants, but in the end, Adam has to know the real you. What it is you want or need, what you care about." He squeezed her shoulder. "Who you are."

Not knowing what else to do, Isabella nodded.

"So for now, if you want to follow Amber, go ahead. Just don't play so long that Adam mistakes your sincerity for an amusing pastime."

Wow. Who knew Noel was so attentive and discerning?

Well, obviously Amber did. "She said I couldn't be easy. That I had to make him work for it."

It surprised her when Noel flushed.

Now wait a minute… Suspicion lifted her brows. "Is that what you're doin' to Amber?" When he looked even guiltier, a grin made her cheeks ache. "You *are*! You're makin' her *work* for it, aren't you?"

Noel walked on.

Delighted, Isabella hustled to catch up to him. "That is so funny."

"No it's not," he said.

"But this is great. Amber, caught in a game of her own makin'." She clapped her hands. "Totally great."

Pivoting to face her, Noel opened his mouth, hesitated, and clamped it shut again. "Just think about what I said, okay?"

"Oh, I definitely will. And thank you." This time as they started off, Isabella hugged his arm and even put her head on his biceps. A nice, solid biceps, she noticed. "You're a good man, Noel Poet. Whatever you do to catch Amber, I hope you catch her right and tight."

Little by little, Noel smiled and relaxed. "That's the plan." They turned the corner and there were three men drinking beers, playing horseshoes, and laughing loudly. One wore a firefighter's T-shirt, one was an EMT, and the other was Tucker Turley, the sheriff. She knew him well since he'd done plenty of community outreach programs at the school library. Turley was the handsomest of the three, which was saying something since they were all pretty fine. But Isabella knew Amber's cousin Kady was already sweet on him, and besides, he'd never, not once, looked at her with interest, and vice versa.

The men hadn't yet noticed them, and suddenly Isabella wanted to run.

"Cold feet?" Noel asked.

She bit her lip and nodded. "Would it be terrible if I just ducked away before they saw me?"

"No. But I doubt that'd work because Amber will probably bring you right back around to them. You're already here so you might as well talk a minute, right? No harm in that."

Just then Turley said, "Noel, get on over here. We need a fourth to even the teams."

"I have a better idea." Noel gently nudged her forward. "Get Isabella to play." And with that, Noel-the-traitor abandoned her.

"She's on my team," Turley said fast, drawing her in with a long muscled arm.

The other two protested, but after quick introductions and a few jokes, they got to playing. To her surprise, she actually had fun. She'd always known she had a competitive streak, but she rarely had time to indulge it.

After she and Turley won the first game, she tried to excuse herself, but instead she got traded off to the EMT as a "lucky charm," and dang if she wasn't on the winning team again.

That meant the firefighter demanded she join him next, and after three games, three wins, and two beers, she finally got free to return to Adam.

Unfortunately, Lisa and Gray were now in the corn booth, and Adam was nowhere to be found.

He hadn't waited for her.

Maybe Noel was right and she'd blown her chance.

*Well, damn.*

STILL WATERS RUN DEEP. That's what Amber claimed.

Issy wasn't prim or proper, she just respected propriety and knew when to mask her real nature.

A nature, Amber claimed, that would enable Isabella to use him up and then dump him.

Amber wanted to introduce her to a bunch of guys that, given a chance, Adam wouldn't let anywhere near her.

Hell, she might have met every one of those guys last night.

She might have taken one of them to her bed.

A strange red haze filled Adam's gaze until he shook his head.

*No.* He couldn't believe that.

In the small fishing boat, he crossed the lake. The family had a variety of boats and he could have used the inboard, the ski boat, or the pontoon. But Issy had a modest house back in the cove and sometimes, especially during the hottest part of summer, the cove got shallow—meaning dangerous to props.

The fishing boat with the small trolling motor was much better suited for the mossy, narrow passage.

Yesterday, after stupidly listening to Amber, he hadn't waited for Issy.

She wanted to visit other guys? He let her.

But after a mostly sleepless night he'd faced the morning with regrets. So now, regardless of what Amber had told him, Adam intended to talk to Issy.

First on the agenda, finding out what she had or hadn't done.

While he considered numerous possibilities, sweat trickled down the back of his neck and the sun baked his bare shoulders and chest. Even behind his mirrored sunglasses, he had to squint against the morning sunshine reflecting off the placid surface of the calm lake.

This early on a Sunday, few boaters were out to disturb the tranquility. Overhead an eagle soared. Along the shore geese honked at him and a flat, lazy water turtle rested over the rocks. Some fish swam alongside the boat while others leaped, making a splash.

Even with the mosquitoes and heat and the occasional drunk boater, Adam loved spending time on the lake. He could still remember, before his mom and Jordan had married, when Jordan brought them all to visit for the first time. There'd been so many kids and laughing adults. But what had struck him the most was the amount of love. Even as a very young boy, he'd felt it, craved it, and thanks to Jordan marrying his mom and adopting both him and his sister, Lisa, he'd become a part of that amazing family.

Jordan was a good man, a man Adam enjoyed calling Dad. A man to be respected by all. The day Jordan met his mom was the day Adam's life had changed—all for the better. Not that his mom hadn't done all she could. His mom was, and always had been, pretty damned terrific.

But Jordan had opened up a world of new, easier possibilities, and much of that centered around the atmosphere of the lake.

Adam could never get on or near the lake without a sense of coming home...for the first time, and forever.

As he neared the cove, Adam heard talking. Annoyance replaced reminiscing.

Did Issy have company? There were no close neighbors, so unless she talked with fishermen...

*Or maybe she'd kept an overnight guest.*

The possibility locked his teeth so tightly his jaw ached. Watchful, he continued on, unsure what he might see there on her weathered dock. He followed the curving shoreline, passed the concealing trees and shrubs.

And his eyes went wide.

Holy hell.

Peeling off his sunglasses and leaning forward over the hot metal seat, Adam soaked up the sight of Issy in a tiny blue bikini...halfway up a large tree.

Slim thighs straddled a fat branch. As she stretched forward, the strapless top of her suit looked in imminent danger of exposing her. Even as Adam watched, her hair came undone from some messy topknot and tumbled down around her shoulders.

The boat knocked into her dock, shaking Adam from his daze. He killed the engine, grabbed for the handle of the ladder that led into the water, and quickly tied off the nose of the boat. "Issy?"

"Shhh!"

His gaze swept the area and he realized she must've used the picnic table to reach that first branch and from there she'd climbed. She had the long strap of a canvas tote slung over her neck and one shoulder.

The tree hung over the shore, partial roots exposed to the constantly shifting water line. Taking in the picture Issy made with her bared skin and awkward hold, Adam trod across the dock to the land, asking more quietly, "What are you doing?"

"Tryin' to get this poor kitty."

Adam got closer, peered up, but he didn't see a cat.

He saw Issy. Mostly naked. Her legs were shapelier than he'd known, her breasts fuller. And that sexy belly...

At the sound of a loud hiss, Adam sucked in a deep breath and forced his gaze away from her body.

Oh, yeah, there in front of her on the branch was an orange cat. Young. Scrawny. And... "Do I see blood on him?"

"I think so." She reached out her hand. "C'mere kitty, kitty, kitty."

The cat arched up and hissed again.

Now with more insistence, Adam said, "Back away from him, Issy. He's feral. If he attacks, you're coming out of the tree the hard way."

"You think he'd—" Before she could finish the cat raised a paw in warning and gave a low, nearly demonic snarl. "Right. Backin' up." She scooted toward the trunk of the tree and looked down. "Know what, Adam?"

He stared at her thighs and thought about things totally inappropriate to the moment. "What?"

"Gettin' up here was probably a whole lot easier than gettin' down."

In her nervousness, her accent sounded thicker.

Adam cleared his throat; it wasn't his accent getting thick. "You have a ladder, hon?"

"In the shed over there."

"Don't move." With alacrity, he went for the ladder and was back in seconds, propping it against the tree and holding it there.

Issy stared down at him again. "Why don't you go do somethin' else till I'm on solid ground?"

He grinned. "No. I'm going to hold the ladder steady for you."

"But—"

Voice deeper, he insisted, "It's not safe, Issy."

She looked back at the cat, down at the ground, and started grumbling under her breath. She removed the canvas tote and dropped it—which only unveiled more of her stunning body.

Using the lower branches to help her, she maneuvered around. When one naked foot came down and felt around for the first ladder rung, it was all Adam could do not to groan.

Issy had a very sweet behind on her. And that teeny tiny bikini didn't leave much to the imagination. He'd seen skimpy bikinis plenty of times, just never on her. Maybe that was it, the reason his libido surged into overdrive. Usually Isabella dressed modestly. Very ladylike. Pretty.

But she never showed so much skin.

Now that he knew what she hid, how would he ever keep his hands off her?

Each rung she descended brought that pert rump closer to him. Occasionally she used the branches to help.

"What if I hadn't come by?" he thought to ask.

"I'd have figured out somethin'."

With her sweet, lyrical accent, he'd always known she didn't sound like a stodgy librarian. Now he also knew her figure didn't match the stereotypical librarian, either. The woman was flat-out smoking hot.

*"Somethin',"* he said, mimicking her, "like what?"

She paused, looked up at the tree, then at the lake. "I reckon I could've dropped into the water."

"Hell of a drop." When she got close enough, Adam reached for her waist and swung her down the rest of the way. She immediately turned to face him, her chin up so she could see his eyes.

His hands were still on her naked waist, and he felt

the dewiness of her skin, smelled the warmth of her from the hot afternoon sun.

He drew her closer.

She came up to her tiptoes...

Temptation had never looked so good. "Probably not a good idea with a pissed off feral cat in a canvas tote."

Confused, a little hazy, she asked, "What's that?"

"Your idea, about dropping into the lake?"

Her eyes almost crossed. "*That's* what you were ponderin'?" Giving a frustrated groan, Issy dropped her forehead to his chest. "We're here doin' the whole eye thing—or at least I thought we were—and you're contemplatin' ways my plan wouldn't work."

"Not really." Mostly he'd been thinking about saving the cat and then moving on to more rewarding pursuits. Like getting Issy out of that itty-bitty swimsuit.

"You are the most impossible man."

"I'm not the one who was sitting naked in a tree."

She lightly punched his side, then braced her hand on him. Then stroked. "I'm not *nekkid*," she whispered.

God, he loved her accent.

She coasted her open hand to his back, then up his spine. Voice gone husky, she said, "And you're wearin' even less than me."

She was still close, and he copied her caress, teasing the line of her spine—and making his own voice hoarse. "My bottoms cover a whole lot more." And good thing, since her nearness had physically affected him.

Leaning back, she took in his chest and breathed a little faster. "You shouldn't be here."

"Why?" He tensed, and automatically tightened his hold on her. "You're expecting company?"

Quirking a slim brow, she laughed. "Seriously, Adam? Would I look like this for company?"

His attention went over her again, and he inhaled. Softly he said, "Works for me."

She pushed away. "I'm not wearin' make-up."

"I've seen you without make-up plenty of times."

"No you haven't. You've seen me wearin' just the right amount of make-up to look like I'm not wearin' it."

Okay, he didn't understand that. Not at all. Screwing up his face, he said, "Come again?"

"I wear *subtle* make-up. You know, enough to make me look prettier."

With complete sincerity, he said, "You're always pretty."

She rolled her eyes. "Since when?"

Adam stalled. This was one of those tricky female questions, and he hated tricky questions. "Since...always?"

"Uh huh." She crossed her arms, which only further plumped up her breasts. "That's why every time we get too close, you say somethin' inane?"

Giving her a truth, Adam said, "You throw me off my game."

"Your game?"

"With women."

"Ooookay." She switched her weight from one foot to the other, as if settling in. "Let's hear it."

Still looking at her hips, he said, "It, what?"

"How I throw you off."

This he could answer, no problem. "You're different from other women." How he wanted her was different. How she affected him.

How she burned him up.

"I'm waitin'." She even tapped her bare foot to the ground. "Expound on that, why doncha?"

"Okay, sure." This part proved more difficult. "You're mature."

After a three-second blank stare, she lifted the back of her wrist to her forehead and slumped against the tree. "My, my, my," she said, and with her accent it sounded like *mah, mah, mah*. "Such heated praise. I do believe I might swoon."

Adam took his time looking at her body in the blue bikini. It had little pink flowers on it and looked both feminine and somehow vintage. With his gaze on the gentle curve of her belly, then her upper thighs, he stepped closer and murmured, "Let me try again." He slid a hand to her waist, and inhaled deeply at the silky warmth of her skin. "You're a smart, independent, confident woman who also happens to be sexy as hell."

Her lips lifted in the slightest of smiles. "Much, much better." She put both hands to his shoulders.

Good.

But he needed to know, so as he skimmed his lips over her cheekbone, he asked, "How'd last night go for you?"

"You left me," she breathed, her eyes sinking shut. "So it was rather disappointin'."

Hope took hold. "No hookups?"

"After chattin' with you?" Her gaze locked with his and she chided, "You should know better."

Just what he'd wanted to hear. "You were gone so long—"

"Sheriff Turly roped me into a coupla games of horseshoes. But I did come back lookin' for you."

"Then I'm sorry I left." More than ready to taste her, Adam leaned down.

Isabella came up.

And the cat dropped behind them with a very annoyed screech.

## *CHAPTER FOUR*

How had she forgotten about the cat? That poor animal was the reason she'd been caught in a tree in her tiniest bathing suit. "I'm a terrible person," she murmured as she took the tote bag and slowly knelt to face the cat.

"No, you're not," Adam told her, and then, "Let me."

"You as good as your daddy?" Jordan Sommerville was known to whisper a cow to sleep, or talk a dog through labor. The man had an amazing ability with soothing animals.

"No one is." Adam came down to one knee beside her. "But I've helped Dad plenty of times, so maybe I can manage. It'd help if we had something to feed him."

Giving her unspoken agreement, Issy moved back.

Adam ignored the tote bag and began speaking softly to the cat.

"Be right back," she whispered, and took off in a jog for the house. She ran in the back door, down the hall and to her closet where she grabbed a gigantic T-shirt that she dropped over her head. She raced back to the kitchen, rummaged in her fridge and finally found some cheese. It'd have to do. She hurried back to Adam...but pulled up short when she saw him sitting cross-legged on the ground, the cat lifting up to Adam's outstretched hand to be petted.

*Awww...* Right then and there, her heart completely

melted. No man should look that mouthwateringly good and also be so caring for animals. That's what she called overkill in the appeal department.

In a barely-there whisper, she asked, "What should I do?"

"Come in here on my other side—slowly—and have the food ready."

As she literally tiptoed, she whispered, "All I had was cheese. I'm not much for lunchmeat or hot dogs or any of that nasty stuff."

"Cheese will work." As she eased down beside him, Adam added, "And hot dogs are not nasty."

The cat watched her warily, braced to run, so she didn't debate the point with him. "How'd you get him to trust you so quickly?"

Adam now had his hand repeatedly coasting down the length of the cat's back, all the way to the tip of his tail. "I repeated some of the things I've heard Dad say, in the way he usually says them. It's worked before on kids at the school, but I'd never tried it on a feral cat."

"You sure he's feral?"

"I think so. But also desperate. She's way too skinny—"

"She?"

Just then the cat high-stepped away from them, tail up as Adam stroked her. Isabella looked, made a face, and said, "I don't see anythin'."

Amusement curved his mouth. "That's the point."

"Oh."

"Anyway, she's got a few superficial injuries, and she needs to eat more. And I'm pretty sure she has fleas."

That sounded horrible, all of it, and Isabella's heart broke just a little. "Poor baby."

"I suggest we try to get her in a crate, then we can take her to Dad. He'll fix her up."

We? Did he mean now? Starting to worry, she asked, "And then what?"

He rolled a shoulder. "Then you have a cat."

She considered it, and liked the idea. "What does that entail, exactly?"

Adam gave her a quick, searching look. "You've never had a pet?"

"No."

His expression softened, almost as if he felt sorry for her.

That didn't offend her because she also thought it was pretty sad that she'd never had a pet to love.

"Hmm...let's see. She could get all her medical treatment right away with Dad. Then you'll need a cat box, for sure. Regular brushings to help her stay groomed. Food, fresh water, the occasional treats... Overall cats are pretty independent. And given this one has been raised outside, I doubt you'd be able to keep her in."

Issy nodded, but said, "You mentioned your dad?"

"He's a vet."

"Right, I know that." He was the most respected vet in three counties. "But don't we need an appointment?"

Moving slowly so he wouldn't spook the cat, Adam lifted a hip and retrieved his cell phone. Using only his thumb, he cleared a passcode, pulled up a number, and put through the call.

A second later, Jordan Sommerville answered.

Adam explained the situation, checked the time on his phone, and said to Issy, "We don't need an appointment."

"Oh." For some reason, she blushed. "Um...good."

He went back to listening, nodded, and asked her, "Lunch with my dad okay by you?"

Lunch. With his *father*.

When she hesitated, Jordan said something else into the phone. Adam half smiled. "Dad said he's buying."

What in the world? What did any of that mean? And why would his father want to have lunch with her?

Confused, she asked, "What about the cat?"

"Dad will keep her overnight. We can grab a bite after he treats her."

Clearly she'd been out-maneuvered, she just didn't know why. Willing to play along, she pasted on a smile. "That sounds lovely. Thank you."

Adam listened to his dad again, nodded a few more times, and finally ended the call by saying, "If by some chance I don't catch her, I'll call you back."

Catch her? After that odd exchange, Adam turned his head, lifted a brow, and smiled at Isabella.

She wondered if he meant the cat, or her.

ISSY DIDN'T HAVE a crate so the cat was in a cardboard box and she wasn't happy about it. Catching her had been easy. Issy had put more food in the box and in the cat went. When he'd closed the flaps, though, she'd flipped out and hadn't settled down since.

Now changed into white jean shorts and a pretty sky blue top, Issy drove them to town in her small compact car. She swallowed repeatedly, winced at the cat's mournful cries, and cringed when it attempted to attack the box.

Adam had secured the box with rope and held it on

his lap. He didn't want to take any chances on having a furious, feral cat loose in the small enclosed space.

"Shh, shh," he said. "It's okay, girl. Dad's anxious to meet you, and I promise you'll like him."

Looking very unsure, Isabella spared him a quick glance. "You *are* talkin' to the cat, right?"

He looked her over, from her tensed shoulders to her smooth thighs and everywhere in between, then said only, "It applies to you both." For as long as he'd known her, Issy had exuded confidence and competence. Now, though, she looked out of her realm.

"Adam?"

"Hmm?"

Her slim throat worked as she swallowed. "How come your father wanted to have lunch?"

He fibbed and said, "You're saving a cat. Dad respects that, so he'd like to meet you." *And he's cagey and intuitive and he knows I'm interested.*

But no reason to share all that when she already seemed so unsure.

Was it because he hadn't given her enough time to put on make-up? Not that Issy needed it, anyway. In the short time they'd been in the yard, she'd gotten some sun and her cheeks, as well as the tip of her nose, were pink. She'd pulled her dark red hair into a loose knot on top of her head, but little silky curls drifted around her temples, her ears, and her nape. Long brown lashes shaded her bright blue eyes and her slim brows continually drew together, telling him whenever she fell into puzzling thought.

Adorable.

Sexy.

And he wanted her.

Still.

*More.*

"Talk to the cat," she ordered. "You make me nervous when you stare."

Instead of looking away, he asked, "What's on your agenda after lunch?"

"Reckon I'll go to a pet store to grab some supplies. When she comes home, I need to be prepared."

After clawing a hole in the side of the box, the cat pressed one eye to it and stared at Issy. Or more like glared.

She gulped and gripped the wheel tighter.

Adam couldn't help but laugh. "I promise she'll settle down. But like I said, she might never be an inside cat. Which just means you'll have to be extra diligent about keeping fresh water and food available outside, watching for ticks and fleas, and keeping her treated."

They pulled into the lot of his dad's clinic. Despite being a Sunday, several cars were there. One Sunday a month the clinic spayed and neutered strays—this must be the day.

Issy parked, then hustled around to his side of the car. All the way in, she fussed and fluttered around as if wanting to help but unsure what to do.

"Take a breath," Adam told her. "It's going to be fine."

But like listening to a baby cry, hearing the cat's forlorn meowing kept her frantic.

A half-dozen neighbors sat in the waiting room, some with dogs, some with cats. They all stared as Adam and Issy came in. Being it was such a small county, he had no doubt Buckhorn would soon be alive with gossip that the middle school librarian was with the gym teacher.

And truthfully, that suited him just fine.

After only a few minutes they were shown to a room, but then waited another fifteen minutes before his dad could join them.

Issy heard him before they saw him and she went on alert. Watching her watch the door, Adam saw her eyes go a little wider, her lips part slightly...

*Why did every little thing seem so sexy?*

Jordan stepped in with a smile. "Adam, Isabella. Sorry you had to wait."

Issy jumped to her feet in a rush. "Dr. Sommerville, thank you. It's obvious you're busy and I appreciate you makin' the time to see us."

Without slowing down, his dad smiled at her, took her hands, and smiled some more. "My pleasure, I promise."

Issy's "deer in the headlights" stillness amused Adam. He said again, "Breathe, honey. It's going to be okay."

His dad released her and turned his knowing gaze on Adam.

Adam, well used to his dad's ways, didn't blink an eye. But Issy, hands locked together, frowned.

After a slow smile, Jordan's focus went to the cat. "The little lady isn't happy."

Seeing Issy's expression, Adam almost laughed. *The cat,* he mouthed to her, then grinned when she blushed.

Adam set the box on a metal table and stepped back to let his dad do his thing.

He did it really well.

"Easy now, sweetheart. It's all right." Jordan kept talking, nonsense mostly, soft words to sooth the cat.

As she listened, Issy's eyes went heavy—as if mesmerized. His dad often had that effect. He could talk to a buzzard and make it coo. Many times his effect had carried over to humans, especially female humans.

His mom sure hadn't been immune.

When Jordan opened the box, Issy backed up next to Adam, expecting the worst after all the cat's snarling complaints.

Instead, as his dad lifted her out and cradled her close, all you could hear were her purrs.

"That's amazin'," Issy breathed.

"Dad has his ways," Adam murmured.

"I'd heard, but I'd never seen." Still watching Jordan, she let out a breath. "You have a true gift, Dr. Sommerville."

"Call me Jordan," he murmured, and twenty minutes later, he had the cat happily settled in a roomy crate with soft bedding and dishes of food and water.

"Tomorrow I'll get the results of the blood tests," his dad told them. "Once she's better rested, we'll treat her for fleas and any other pests. Do you have a name for her that I can enter in the medical records?"

Issy, still watching the cat with a very soft expression, shook her head. "I'm sorry, but I hadn't even thought about it."

"You're keeping her?"

She nodded. "Yes."

Adam saw that she'd already won over his dad, but that decision definitely cinched the deal. Jordan Sommerville was a sucker for anyone who cared for his beloved animals.

Satisfied, Adam said, "We'll come up with something over lunch." He slipped his arm around her, a move his dad noted, just as Adam had intended. He'd get his dad on his side, and some of the townsfolk.

Knowing Amber was out to set Isabella up with other men, staking a claim—even a temporary one—seemed like a very good idea.

Isabella wanted to melt under the table.

The second they'd walked into the diner, Sawyer and Morgan Hudson, Adam's uncles, had waved them over to their four-seat table. A waitress was beckoned to bring a fifth chair and now they were all squeezed together.

How in the world had she gotten into this situation?

Three of the four patriarchs of Buckhorn were currently smiling at her, and she just plain didn't understand it.

While they waited for their food, the men all engaged her in conversation. She knew each of them, of course. You couldn't live in Buckhorn and not know them.

As the town doctor, Sawyer ran a private practice out of his home, something he'd been doing since the day he got his medical license. In his mid-sixties, silver tinged his black hair and smile lines emphasized his chocolate brown eyes. He was still a very handsome man with an athletic build that she knew he'd gotten from working on the family property whenever he didn't have patients to see.

Morgan, only a little younger than Sawyer, remained a beast of a man, broad in the shoulders and thick in the chest. He had the same silver-tipped black hair but with vivid blue eyes that seemed to see *everything*. He'd once been sheriff but was now the mayor, and very involved in community service.

Jordan, the youngest of the three in his late fifties, had a very different look. Sun-kissed brown hair and deep green eyes. The only thing he shared with the others was his height and athletic build.

The entire clan—all of Adam's family—were physical specimens, beyond nice, and respected by everyone.

Figured the man she wanted most would be related to the town's leading family. Sighing, she accepted that she'd gone into it with her eyes wide open, well aware of his relatives. When she thought of Adam, it just plain didn't matter what complications there might be.

"So you're adopting a cat?" Sawyer asked.

"More like the cat adopted me," she said. "But yes, I'm happy to keep her."

"We have a project going to help feral cats," Morgan told her. "Where there's one, there's usually more. So if you see them, let me know."

Going cautious, Issy asked, "What would you do?"

Sawyer laughed. "Not what you might be thinking. No one in my family would take part in destroying an animal."

Letting the tension out of her shoulders, Isabella smiled. "Good to know."

"We TNR," Morgan explained. "Trap, neuter, release."

Fascinated, she asked, "How exactly does that work?"

"We get them treated, spayed or neutered," Sawyer said, "then notch an ear so we can recognize them later in case they get trapped again. Some can be domesticated, but some prefer to stay wild."

Jordan added, "Cats are more capable than you'd

think. As long as they aren't growing their colony, they survive."

Adam's thigh brushed hers as he shifted toward her. "You know Nadine, Shohn's wife?"

"Yes." She cleared her throat to take the squeak out of her voice. "She runs that adorable pet hotel."

"Well, she's helping a lot. Uncle Gabe built her a huge structure where quite a few cats can live until they're adopted. It gives them partial access to the yard, and plenty of ways to climb. Uncle Gabe started calling it Nadine's 'cat sanctuary' and the name stuck."

His uncle, Gabe Kasper, was the only one currently not on site. As the youngest of the brothers, Gabe had once cultivated quite the reputation as a wild hedonist. But now, as a man happily settled into the domestic life with a wife he adored and three grown daughters of his own, the rep was merely a tool for his family to tease him.

His daughters were all sinfully gorgeous like him, but feminine, with pale blond hair and big blue eyes and the same flirtatious nature as their dad. Since he was the town's best handyman, Isabella had once hired him to do some roof repairs, so she knew him a little better than the others.

Worried about the feral cats, she asked, "What if they never get adopted?"

"Then they'll live out the rest of their lives at Nadine's," Jordan told her. "Safe and cared for, but of course, it's not an ideal situation."

"Those poor babies." She hadn't even met the other cats, but already her heart broke for them.

"The key," Adam said, "is to get as many of them

fixed as we can. That'll at least slow down the population."

"Is there any way I can help?"

All the men grinned at her, and even more odd than that was Adam's look of approval...or maybe even pride—though that didn't make any sense. But then he draped a possessive arm over her shoulders, and the rest shared a knowing look.

"All right," Isabella said, flattening her hands on the table and glaring at each man, especially Adam. "*What* is goin' on here?"

## *CHAPTER FIVE*

WITH PROPITIOUS TIMING, the waitress brought their food, interrupting what looked to be a small explosion in Issy's attitude. Course, she hadn't missed the way his relatives kept sizing her up. Although favorably, it still had to be a little disconcerting.

Leaning in, Adam whispered near her ear, "Relax. They just like you. That's all."

"It's more than that," she muttered back. "I'm startin' to feel like a virgin sacrifice."

Morgan guffawed, making Issy go red and drawing the attention of other diners.

Sawyer elbowed him. "I'm sure you weren't supposed to hear that."

"Not like we're deaf," Morgan said, defending himself.

Jordan smiled at her. "We're aging, but haven't yet lost our faculties."

Issy picked up a giant loaded burger that matched almost exactly what the rest of them had ordered. After saying, "You're all outrageous, that's what you are," she took a big bite.

And damn if that didn't earn even more approval from the elders.

Morgan opened his mouth, and Adam rushed to say, "You're going to scare her off. You realize that, right?"

"Is that so?" Jordan asked, munching on a fry while scrutinizing Issy. "You quick to turn tail and run?"

"No." She took another bite, eyed them all while she chewed, and after a drink of her cola, she asked, "Mind tellin' me why I'm being sized up, though?"

This time there was no shushing Morgan. "The boy's been hanging with all the wrong kind of girls."

Smiling with false sweetness, Issy chided him. "I presume you mean women?"

"I'll call 'em what I like, and sometimes, with Adam's preferences, *girl* is more apt."

"Mostly vacationers," Jordan said with a lot of meaning.

Issy cocked a brow. "What's wrong with vacationers?"

"They're temporary."

"Ah." She looked more confused than ever.

"You're different," Sawyer tossed out.

"I'm definitely local, if that's what you mean."

"Sure, that—and more."

Adam watched her so closely, he caught the glare she flashed his way. "You mean I'm *mature*."

So she was still smarting over that? Adam hid a grin. It hadn't been one of his finer moments, but damn, Issy threw him off—in wonderful ways.

"We mean," Morgan said, apparently speaking for all of them, "you've got more going for you than just good looks."

A blush crawled up her neck all the way to her forehead.

Jordan slowly smiled. "You know you're attractive, right?" Then to Adam, "You've told her she's attractive?"

That, and more, but he only said, "Yup."

Issy appeared momentarily nonplussed, then she let out a breath and pasted on a smile. "Thank you?"

The men all glared at him. "You're *sure* you've told her?" Morgan demanded.

Giving up, Adam shrugged. "Let's just say I've been less than smooth in my compliments."

That made his dad's smile widen, and the three of them shared more elbow nudges.

"Now what?" Issy demanded. "What's with all the…" She jabbed her elbows left and right, mimicking them and making them all laugh.

It was Sawyer who spoke up this time. "It takes a certain woman to throw a man off his game. We know the truth of that from experience."

Adam cocked a brow. "You're talking about when you met Honey?"

"And when Morgan met Misty," Sawyer confirmed.

"And when I met your mother," Jordan added. "When you were only four years old and hiding behind her knee."

Adam scowled. "Now wait a minute…"

His protest caused another round of guffaws.

"Oh, please tell me," Issy said, shooting him a teasing smile. "I'd love to hear about Adam as a boy."

That opened the floodgates, and the jibes poured free.

Oddly enough, now that Adam was out of sorts, Issy smiled and tucked into her food with renewed hunger, eating while they regaled her with goofy stories of him as an awkward kid.

But they spoke with unmistakable fondness, and every so often Issy sighed and smiled at him. Huh.

So his uncles and dad were pretty good at this sort of thing. He should have realized that sooner.

When they finally wound down, the food was nearly gone.

"You must have a fast metabolism." Sawyer nodded at her nearly empty plate. "You don't look big enough to have eaten all that."

"I guess." She munched down a remaining fry. "I don't do well with idle time, which is why I was gonna spend my off day pullin' weeds down by the shore before I spotted that poor cat in the tree."

"You pull weeds in your bikini?" If so, Adam thought, then it was a wonder all the fishermen didn't congregate in that particular cove.

"Maybe," she drawled in that fetching accent of hers, "you failed to notice the heat. It's downright steamy."

"I'm sure he noticed," Jordan murmured.

"He's slow," Morgan said, "but not stupid."

With a growl, Adam said, "Maybe you guys should quit helping me now."

"Is that what they're doin'?" Issy pointed a fry at them and laughed. "Y'all don't make it easy to tell. But I can assure you, Adam needs no help."

That pleased the elders, but Adam wondered what the hell it meant.

Morgan cocked a brow. "He doesn't, huh?"

"Nope."

Sawyer looked at Jordan, who only shrugged.

Adam waited for her to expound on that, and instead she finished off the last pickle and two fries on her plate.

Amused, Morgan asked, "Dessert?"

"Not for me, thank you." She looked inquiringly at the others.

His dad declined. "I need to get back to the clinic."

"And I'll have patients showing up soon," Sawyer said.

"Then I suppose I should get back to pullin' my weeds." She wrinkled her nose. "It's the truth I've let things get overgrown. My schedule just stays so busy."

"Dating?" Sawyer asked.

Issy laughed and laughed, as if that was the funniest thing ever.

Adam didn't see the humor. She could have a date every night if she wanted. If Amber had her way, it might happen still.

To keep his dad and uncles from getting the wrong impression, Adam explained, "She's the school librarian, I think you all know that. But she also volunteers extra hours at the school. Isabella is great with kids, especially the kids who struggle with learning disabilities. She goes out of her way to ensure they all can read."

Finally done with her chuckles, Issy said, "Sometimes it's just a matter of findin' the right book for the right child. They're not all on the same level, and for a certainty, they don't have the same interests."

The men all agreed, alternately praising her and asking questions.

It struck Adam that he had a lot of reasons to be proud of Issy. Not just her beautiful face or understated sexiness, or even her sweet nature. She had... substance.

*Real* substance.

The kind you didn't mind showing off to your family.

And if he told her that, she'd no doubt mock him again.

He'd known other admirable women, he reminded himself. A lawyer, social worker, a CEO. Smart women. Beautiful women.

But somehow, none of them had been the whole package; smart, educated, but still very approachable. Caring about kids and animals alike. Bold one minute and reserved the next. Sexy without seeming to know it, and sweet even when giving him hell. She had a sharp wit and a generous heart.

"We've lost him," Sawyer murmured.

"Coming to grips," Jordan guessed.

"There y'all go again," Issy said, her accent getting more noticeable. "Sayin' things I don't understand."

"Tell you what," Morgan said. "Why don't you come by for dinner Sunday? It'll give you a chance to get to know us all better."

"We grill out," Jordan explained. "There'll be swimming, boating, horseshoes and badminton."

"Shohn and Nadine will be there," Sawyer added. "Garrett and Zoey. Amber, too."

Morgan nodded. "Misty and Honey are leaving it as an open invitation, so more of the young folk will probably show up."

Adam felt his dad watching him, maybe waiting for him to protest, to make excuses. But hell, he wanted Amber to see Issy with him, to know she could quit with her match-making efforts. At least for now.

At least until…when?

Adam didn't know, and there was no reason he had to decide this minute. "What do you say, Issy?"

Big blue eyes stared at him with surprise. "Well, I…"

"You'll have the kitty back by then, and could bring her along. I'll give her a follow-up," Jordan offered. "Let you know how she's settling in."

And just that easily, Issy nodded. "All right. Thank you."

Something eased in Adam's chest. He needed more time with her. More than lunch, more than dinner with his enormous, pushy, intrusive family around. *Private* time.

He glanced at the clock on the diner wall. Still plenty of time for him to make a move.

With any luck, he wouldn't botch it this time.

ISABELLA STOOD IN her driveway, uncertain what to do now. After a quick trip to the pet store for supplies, they'd ridden home in an odd silence with Adam watching her intently, smiling every so often.

Maybe planning, though she wasn't sure about that part. They'd each exited the car in the same quiet way...and now what?

She felt out of her depth, and very uncertain on what should happen next. "I guess you need to get on home?" She winced after she said it, hearing the question, and the hope.

"Is that a hint for me to leave?"

"No!"

His gaze heated and somehow sensual, Adam closed in on her. "I'm not in a rush." He cupped her shoulders and drew her against him. "What about you?"

Heaven help her, the man could scatter her thoughts with a touch.

Feeling lame and hesitant—and a little like warmed gelatin—she gestured with a limp hand toward the back of her house and the waiting shoreline. "Well, after I put away the cat's stuff, I was gonna get to those weeds…"

"Planning to put your suit back on?" His chocolate brown eyes stared down at her, making it difficult for her to breathe.

Pleased that he'd liked her suit—and her in it—she lifted one shoulder. "Maybe." *Definitely*, if it enticed him into staying.

He grinned, and it made him so handsome she wanted to go on tiptoe and kiss him silly. In fact…

Heartbeat racing, breathless, she inched up.

"Mind if I stay and help?"

Her gaze went from his mouth to his sexy bedroom eyes. "Help?"

"With your landscaping cleanup."

In a million years, she would never understand him. "You wanna stay and help me pull weeds?"

"Sure."

She shoved back from him. "Are we *ever* thinkin' the same things?"

He laughed. Actually *laughed*.

Oh, that got her irked. "My confusion is funny?" she asked in a deadly whisper.

"The idea that you'd not know what I'm thinking is." He moved close again. "Because I was thinking about how you look in that bathing suit…and how you'd look out of it."

Heat washed over her and it had nothing to do with the broiling sun. "You were?"

He gave a slow nod. "About kissing you. Touching you all over."

So maybe they had been thinking along the same lines.

He tipped up her chin and brushed his mouth over hers.

Holy cow, that was intense. A real toe-curler.

His warm breath feathered her lips when he murmured, "I keep reminding myself that I shouldn't rush things."

Blast. "Why not?"

The corner of his mouth lifted, and his hand slid along her jaw and up to cradle her skull. "Because you still have it in your head that you might want to woo other men."

Her brain was back there on that part about him getting her out of her swimsuit. She shook her head. "What?"

He kissed her again, firmer this time, his mouth moving easily over hers—and seriously, that did *not* help her to get it together.

He smiled down at her. "You've forgotten that you were going to practice your wiles on me?"

It sounded a little familiar...

"Have to admit, Issy," he whispered. "I'm looking forward to it."

Her house was private. They were all alone on the end of the lane, surrounded by a cow pasture on one side, thick woods on the other. *Go for it*, Isabella decided.

After licking her tingling lips, she went on tiptoe and looped her arms around his neck. "So how's this for wooin'?" Her breasts brushed his chest and her thighs touched his.

"Pretty damned good." He stared at her mouth. "Any guy who walks away at this point isn't into women."

"And this?" She brushed her nose along his warm throat, inhaling the potent scent of his skin, teasing him and teasing herself. Sensation curled through her as she kissed the warm flesh of his neck, a light touch at first, then with her lips parted, damper, hotter. She tasted him with her tongue, lightly bit him with her teeth.

His hands clenched on her hips, bringing her body into fuller contact with his so that she felt him, all of him.

Her pulse leapt. She wanted him *so much*. Not just for tonight. Not only for a weekend.

But *forever*.

*Have to start somewhere*, she told herself. Sex, right now, would sure get things started!

Licking her way up to his ear, she nipped his earlobe, brushed her lips over his jaw, touched the corner of his mouth, and...found herself being ravenously kissed.

*Nice.*

As her feet left the ground, she held on to him, loving the hungry way he took her mouth, the plunging of his tongue, his hot breath, how he groaned low in his throat.

Taking her by surprise and leaving her cold, he suddenly set her back on her feet, and their bodies no longer touched.

Dazed, she blinked and said, "Wha..?"

Adam stared along the drive, cursed, and grabbed her hand. "Come on."

Still disoriented, she couldn't get her feet working. "What...where..?"

"You have a visitor, honey. And we both need a minute before greeting them."

## *CHAPTER SIX*

ADAM HAD A hell of a time getting his heartbeat to slow back to a semi-normal pace. He was hard, almost shaking with lust, and it didn't make any sense.

Issy had only kissed him. He'd been kissed before.

And sure, her scent intoxicated him. But most women smelled good. And were soft. And sweet.

How was she so different?

How did she affect him so strongly?

At the side of the house, his knees locked, his breath strained, he stared down at her.

She stared back. "Are you okay?"

A deep breath didn't really help, but it at least gave him a second more to think. A car door slammed and the sound of conversation—*a male voice*—carried from the driveway to where they stood.

Possessive urges swamped him, narrowing his vision until all he could see was Issy. Urgency kicked his heart back into a racing beat. He hadn't yet had her. He damn straight didn't want some yokel stepping ahead of the line.

"Adam?" she whispered, her expression growing wary.

He cupped one hand to her jaw, ran his thumb over her swollen bottom lip. "Did you invite someone over?"

Leaning her cheek into his palm, eyes closed, she whispered, "No."

The relief stayed just out of reach. "Then who—"

They both heard Amber's laugh.

Damn it. Umbrage stiffened his spine. *His busybody cousin had brought a man to Issy's house!* What was she, a pimp?

Issy patted his chest, turned to kiss his palm, then whispered, "Just a second, okay?" She crept to the side of the house to peek around, taking care not to be seen.

Expression incredulous, her brows pinched, she ducked back and whispered to Adam, "It's the EMT I met at the carnival."

No, he decided. Not happening.

Yet as Issy pondered the situation, his indignation swelled.

She looked up at him. "You could sneak back to your boat and—"

"I'm not going anywhere."

That had Isabella tipping her head in a curious way. "If your cousin sees you here, how will you explain?"

*I'm first in line.* But no, of course he couldn't say that. It sounded horrible. She wasn't a prize to be won. She was a beautiful, intelligent woman who just happened to make him insanely crazed with lust.

And seriously, he didn't want there to be a line. Thinking about any other guys sidling up to her for any intimate reason—even a kiss—left him infuriated.

Only he didn't have the right to be infuriated. At the moment, he didn't have any rights at all.

Probably time to change that.

If he could.

"Yoohoo, Adam," she teased softly, waving a hand in front of his face. "You still in there?"

"I'll tell her about the cat."

One brow going up, Issy said softly, "Okay. So then why are you still here?"

*Because I need you.*

"She'll ask, Adam. You know that."

Before he could answer, he needed to know. "What are you going to do?"

"Get rid of him as quickly, but nicely, as I can."

There'd been no hesitation, and he believed her. He was a lucky guy.

Amber's voice reached them as she called out, "Isabella?"

"She's comin' this way," Issy said urgently. "Make up your mind."

Adam grabbed her in for a quick, firm kiss. He wanted her to remember he was waiting. "I'll stay out of sight. Soon as they're gone, you and I need to talk."

"We do," she agreed, coming in for yet another fast peck. "And I'll go first." Then she slipped around the house, catching Amber just before she would have busted them.

"Hey, Amber," Issy said in her soft drawl. "Sorry, I was down by the lake."

Adam stayed put, content to listen in.

"Just you?" Amber asked.

Adam recognized the tone. Amber already knew he was with Issy. How she knew was anyone's guess. But for sure, she knew.

"Uh-huh. So what's up?"

Glee sounded in Amber's tone when she said, her voice all silky, "You remember Wayne?"

"Of course. How are you, Wayne?"

For the next five minutes, Adam ground his teeth while listening to the byplay between Wayne and Issy.

Wayne wanted her. That much was clear. The way he spoke, how he laughed… Adam recognized the signs. Repeatedly Issy came up with excuses for why she couldn't get together, and repeatedly, Wayne found a new way to ask.

Coming on all hot and heavy, Wayne told her that he'd always been interested but she gave off "don't touch" vibes.

Ha! Adam glanced around at the guy with smug victory. Isabella had all but insisted that *he* touch her. That had to mean a lot.

"I'm sorry," Issy said for the tenth time, "but I—"

"C'mon," Wayne interrupted smoothly. "At least give me a chance."

Adam was about to intervene when from behind him, Amber whispered, "You big fraud."

He jumped a foot.

Damn it, he'd been so fixated on Issy's conversation with Wayne, he hadn't realized that Amber was no longer on the scene, and he hadn't even heard her approach behind him.

He jerked around to face her and caught her enormous grin. Pointing toward the back patio, he gave a silent order and with a shrug, Amber sashayed that way.

"So what are you doing?" Amber whispered.

"None of your business."

"Ooh, so it's that type of visit." She patted his shoulder, sharing her pity. "And right in the middle of things, Wayne moves in."

"He didn't 'move in'," Adam corrected with annoyance. "You dragged him here."

"Now, Adam," she chastised. "The man is more than willing. Trust me, he did not have to be coerced."

If he didn't stop grinding his teeth, he'd turn them to powder. "I thought you liked me."

She laughed quietly and gave him a hug. "I *love* you, silly. But I didn't know you were that interested." Holding him back, she asked, "You're saying you are?"

Adam opened his mouth—then snapped it shut. He wouldn't make confessions to his cousin before he even made them to Issy. "I'm saying you need to stop the stud parade. She doesn't need your help."

"Stud parade," Amber mused. "I like that."

Yeah, Issy might like it, too—if he didn't nix it real quick. "You have to stop." But he knew she wouldn't. Amber was like a tsunami. Once she got started, all you could do was brace yourself.

"Aw, what's wrong? Tell Amber all about it."

He scowled. "Don't talk about yourself in third person. You aren't the queen."

She laughed a bit loudly, and slapped her hand over her mouth.

Adam took her shoulders. "Amber, seriously." He bent his knees to meet her gaze at eye level. "I need you to give me a little time with her."

She sobered quickly. "Do you care about her?"

He did, but how much? Because he wasn't ready to figure it out just yet, he said instead, "I'm working it out. *We're* working it out. But it makes it tough when you keep tossing single men her way."

"Afraid of the competition, huh?"

For what Issy wanted? Yes. He might already be too involved, but as far as he knew, she wanted to sow wild oats.

If she only sowed them with him, that could work.

But with Amber offering up so many alternatives-

"I'll give you a week," Amber said decisively. "Let's say...the picnic next weekend? Dad told me that he invited her to join us and that you further coerced her. So she'll be there, right?"

Um... "Yes?" Why did it still feel like Amber plotted his failure? It shouldn't have scared him, but determination glittered in her eyes and it never failed to set him on edge.

"Terrific." She put her finger in his face and leveled a firm look on him. "One week, Adam."

"That's not much time..."

She rolled her eyes. "You've known her five years, for crying out loud. Seven days is more than enough time for you to decide if you're interested in friendship, a fling or more." Triumphant, pleased with her own plans, she smiled, hugged him tight, and walked away.

From a safe distance Adam followed and heard her say, "Sorry, Wayne, we need to get going."

Wayne sputtered. "But I was—"

"I know," Amber crooned, her voice laden with sympathy. "I think Isabella has made other plans, though, so there's no point in dragging this out. Come on. We'll talk about other prospects while I drive you home." Truck doors closed and the engine revved. Amber yelled, "I'll see you this weekend, Issy. Make the most of your week!"

As her truck disappeared, Adam stepped out. Having a timeframe laid out pushed his fevered urgency to the breaking point. He needed Issy. Today.

*Right now.*

She had her back to him, watching the dust settle after Amber's truck departed. Sensing her melancholy, he stepped close to her, waiting, hoping she'd turn to him, touch him again.

The heat of her small body lured him, and he cupped his hands over her shoulders. Her scent filled his head and, unable to resist, he drifted his nose along her nape. "Issy?"

Resting against him, she whispered, "That talk?"

"Yes?"

"Do you think we could put it off for...oh, I don't know." Her voice deepened. "Maybe an hour or so?"

He had one week and he didn't plan to waste a single second. Gently turning her to face him and tugging her into full body contact, he brushed his mouth over her soft lips. "We can do anything you want."

"Perfect."

Adam held his breath.

"Let's get to those weeds."

WAIST DEEP IN the water, her hair pinned atop her head with sweat trickling down her temples and across her shoulders, Isabella cleared away weeds growing along the rock retaining wall. With every heartbeat she was aware of Adam a few yards up the shoreline, shirtless, his fair hair haloed by the sunshine, his shoulders bronzed.

At first, after Amber and Wayne had left, Adam had seemed surprised that she didn't want to go straight to bed with him. She *did* want to, but that would be nuts. They needed to talk.

About so much.

She didn't understand herself, and it made her sigh—which drew Adam's attention.

He glanced her way, pausing to swipe a forearm over

his brow. "Everything okay, Issy?" With his reflective sunglasses in place, she couldn't read his expression.

But she saw his small smile.

"Yes." Sort of.

She couldn't stop thinking about Wayne, about how bizarrely insistent he'd been. He was a good-looking man with a noble job where he helped others. Tall. Charming. Bold.

But he wasn't Adam, so none of that mattered.

"You need a break?" he asked. "I can finish up here."

Talk about noble...the man had thought they would have sex. She'd seen that in his gaze. But when she suggested work instead, he hadn't balked. And now he offered to let her off the hook while he finished alone.

Isabella shook her head and wondered why she kept dragging her feet.

It wouldn't get any easier.

In a lot less time, Adam had accomplished quite a bit more than she did, so they'd already finished pulling the weeds around the yard. Once they finished along the retaining wall, they'd be done.

She heard a splash and turned to where Adam was last. All that remained was his sunglasses on the rock wall. Water moved around her and a second later he broke the surface right in front of her.

Lake water slicked back his hair, emphasizing his dark sinner's eyes. His scent was more pronounced, deliciously so. Issy touched his damp chest hair. "Guess you needed the break?"

"I need a kiss more." He brought her against his incredible body, making her gasp as his now cooled skin met her heated body. "What do you say?"

Nodding, Issy looked at his mouth and whispered, "I say yes." Always, yes.

She *loved* kissing Adam.

As he slowly lowered his head, his smile faded. He skimmed his lips along her jaw, up to her ear. "Jesus, you smell good."

She clutched at his shoulders. "You do, too."

He kissed her sensitive throat, and one hand dipped under the water to stroke her back, down her waist, and over her hip.

He leaned back to see her as he palmed her backside in the wet bathing suit bottoms. His eyes turned darker, heavy-lidded. When he hoisted her against him, she naturally put her legs around his waist.

Wet fingertips trailed over her shoulder to her throat, then along the top edge of her bathing suit top. "You ever had sex in the lake, Issy?"

Heartbeat thundering, she shook her head.

"You'd love it," he promised huskily. "And this cove is private enough to make it possible."

Scandalized, titillated, she whispered, "You mean..?"

He smiled and lightly kissed her mouth. "Not this time."

What a tease! "Why not?" Now that he'd said it, she wanted it, damn it.

"Because our first time I want to see you. Every inch of you. And that's not possible with half your body hidden in the water."

"Oh." Okay, that sounded pretty good too, because if Adam could see all of her, she'd be able to see all of him. A win-win.

Those teasing fingers played with one strap of her

bra-top, ramping up her anticipation until finally he slid it down her left shoulder, down, down, until he could carefully scoop her breast free.

They both groaned.

Adam didn't kiss her—he was too busy looking at her, at the way his rough fingers held her pale breast, how his big thumb teased over her already taut nipple, sending ripples of sharp pleasure straight to her womb.

In a voice gone rough, he said, "I need to taste you, Issy."

Her thighs tightened around him and she watched as his head lowered to her, as his tongue circled, teased, and then as his lips closed over her, sucking gently.

*So* good. So, so *deliciously* good.

Letting her head drop back, she arched her body, bringing their pelvises closer together. Good Lord, she felt the pull of his mouth in amazing places. He readjusted so that the hand holding her bottom could slip into her trunks over her bare flesh. His long fingers searched over her, making her squirm and gasp, before sliding over her slick sex. He didn't press his fingers into her; no, he just teased, over and over, until she felt frenzied and couldn't stop her hips from moving against him.

Lifting his head, he groaned, "I'm on the ragged edge here, Isabella. Tell me you want me."

Words were beyond her. She was already so far gone that it amazed her. She tried to draw a breath but it sounded like a high-pitched cry instead. The water swirled around them.

With wonder, Adam breathed, "Damn," then eased a finger into her, testing her, feeling the slicker wetness of her excitement. "You're close, aren't you, baby?"

Unable to think, she locked one hand in his hair, braced the other on his shoulder. "Adam...*please*," she breathed.

As his gaze searched over hers, it filled with satisfaction. "Whatever you want, honey." Bending back to her breast, he drew her in again, this time not so gently. He worked a second finger into her, keeping them pressed deep as she rolled her hips, moving in the rhythm she needed, ready to break. Close. *So close.*

But before she quite reached that critical peak, the sound of an approaching boat motor caught their attention.

Apparently better able to think than she was, Adam dipped them both lower in the lake, letting the dock hide them.

Gasping every breath, *so* incredibly close, Isabella wanted to cry. Her broken breaths sounded with disappointment and her body throbbed with need.

She hid her face against Adam's neck and struggled to catch her breath.

Adam stroked her back. "I'm sorry, Issy. So damn sorry." He glanced over the dock and cursed. After a quick soft kiss to her mouth, he freed his hands from her and let her feet drop to the muddy bottom of the lake. "Stay here. I'll take care of it."

"Adam?" she whispered.

He paused.

Even though she'd been the one about to climax, he looked as turned on as her. Color slashed his cheekbones and his dark eyes burned.

Isabella swallowed. "You don't want to hide again?"

"No." He tucked a wisp of hair behind her ear. "Never again."

She hadn't expected that, but she nodded. "They already saw you?"

"I don't think so." His hand settled against her cheek. "But I'd just as soon everyone know that I'm here, with you." He kissed her softly. "And why."

Her heart tried to lodge in her throat. "Oh." She wanted to ask why, but said only, "Um... Okay."

Grinning, he said, "How about you keep that agreeable mood? I'll get rid of these guys and get right back to you and then we'll see what else you might agree to."

## *CHAPTER SEVEN*

THE SLIGHT BREAK while Adam spoke to two fishermen gave Isabella a second to think.

She'd been grossly unfair, and she knew it. Without any real honesty between them, she'd roped Adam in, making him think he'd be no more than a sexual fling for her. He assumed they could indulge a brief hookup and then each go about their respective business, interacting at the school in a platonic way as usual, existing in the same small county without a single note of hard feelings.

He had no clue that it would kill her to let him go. He didn't know that, with Amber's help, she'd targeted him specifically.

Noel Poet's words kept ringing in her head: *Don't play so long that Adam mistakes your sincerity for an amusing pastime.*

Physically, she wanted him. No way would she deny him now. But he had to know how she felt.

He deserved the truth.

She loved him, had for a while now, and it was past time he knew it, too.

While Isabella removed the band in her hair and slowly dunked her head beneath the cool water, the two fishermen indulged in idle chitchat with Adam. He appeared to know them, and didn't seem to mind when they made a few assumptions about finding him at her dock.

In fact, he encouraged them to see the truth.

"So you're helping her with yard work?"

"It was as good an excuse as any to hang around," Adam said.

Hearing that, Isabella went still.

The men laughed, wished him luck in winning her over—*ha!*—and finally moseyed on.

But they were no sooner gone than another boat showed up, this time a pontoon with Turley and the fireman she'd met at the carnival. She didn't remember his name, but Adam helped remind her by saying, "Turly, Bear. How ya' doing?"

Bear, that's right. How could she have forgotten that?

"Where's Isabella?" Bear asked.

In a not-so-nice tone, Adam replied, "Why do you ask?"

Turly laughed. "A day late and a dollar short, Bear."

"Is that so?" Bear asked, presumably to Adam since that's who answered. "Did I miss my chance?"

"You never had a chance," Adam told him. "For damn sure, you won't get one now."

Clinging to a dock pier, Isabella blinked. She had no idea how to take that. Staking a claim? On *her*?

But...for how long?

With the brief moment of privacy, she'd gathered a modicum of control. There was no reason to leave Adam to deal with the men on his own, so, after a deep breath, she hoisted herself up to the side of the dock.

As she stood, she said, "Hi, guys."

All three men faced her. A beat of tense silence made her squirm. She tried a smile to put them at ease.

Turly pushed back his sunglasses and whistled.

Bear stared as if he'd never in his life seen a woman in a swimsuit, then swallowed audibly.

For crying out loud. Hers was more modest than many, not that you could tell by his reaction. In fact, the way he stared, she was starting to feel naked when she knew most women on the lake were in skimpier bikinis.

She was trying to think of something to say when Adam appeared in front of her. "If there's nothing else, you guys can get lost."

Finally regaining his wits, Turly burst out laughing.

"Now wait a minute," Bear protested as the boat motor rumbled to life. "Amber said—"

"Amber was obviously wrong," Turly told him, and he took a sharp turn, angling the boat back out of the cove. Bear craned his neck to keep her in his sights, still trying to protest when they disappeared from view.

"That was so odd."

Adam turned to stare down at her. "You just gave Turly a mild heart attack." His hand opened on her waist, his thumb moving over her belly.

"I don't know—"

"You are sexy beyond belief."

Isabella would have denied that, but he kissed her. Not a tentative kiss, but a 'Let's pick up where we left off' hot, wet, involved-tongue kiss.

Clinging to him, she kissed him back, and all the same sensations swamped her, putting her right back on that precipice of release.

Adam inched away to look at her. "Your house?"

he asked hopefully as he trailed his fingertips over her still damp shoulder.

Her house, where they could be alone, where boaters couldn't intrude.

Where she could finally have Adam Sommerville in all the ways she wanted. "Yes," she breathed.

*No, wait.* Not *all* the ways she wanted...because she wanted him forever.

He started to move but she stayed him. "Hold up." God, this was harder than she'd ever imagined. "I need to tell you somethin' first."

"All right." He didn't pressure her, just looped his arms around her waist, studied her face, and waited.

SEEING THE RETICENCE in Issy's expression, Adam frowned. Something wasn't right.

Only a few minutes ago, she'd been ready to come apart from his touch. He'd felt the wetness of her slicking his fingers, felt her heat and the way she clung to him, heard the incredibly sexy sounds she made as her release grew near.

She wanted him, he knew that. Hell, she hadn't been shy about letting him know. But now, when they were finally ready to end the torture, she kept him standing on the dock.

She looked worried, and he didn't like that. When they got together—*and please, let it be now*—he wanted her with him one-hundred percent.

Forcing himself to patience, he asked, "What is it, honey?"

A deep inhalation lifted her breasts. Beautiful, full breasts.

She braced herself—why, he didn't know—and

scooted closer, kissing his chest, his shoulder. "I'm hopin' you don't get mad."

They were ready to have sex; why the hell would he be mad?

"And I hope you don't change your mind. I really, really hope that."

"Change my mind about wanting you? Not going to happen." He needed her. He was so hard he hurt, but now, with this build-up of something, his gut cramped a little. "Whatever it is—"

"I love you," she blurted.

Adam fell back a step and almost went off the side of the dock. Issy grabbed him, helping him regain his balance. He stepped them both forward, away from the edge.

Talking ninety miles a minute, Issy held on to him. "I've loved you for a long time! I'm so sorry I didn't say somethin' earlier. But I was afraid to. I didn't think... that is, I know you don't feel the same."

He opened his mouth—but nothing came out. He needed a second to think.

"*I love you*," she said again, her voice filled with longing. "But I want you, too."

Want, as in sexually? That was good...or was it?

"You're confused," she said, her eyes big and filled with dread. "Of course I understand why. Please, please know that I don't expect anything. I mean, I want things. I hope for things. But for this—" She gestured between them. "—that's a given, okay?"

Stupidly, he shook his head. "This?"

"Sex. Us. We can do that regardless. We *will* do that. I mean, I *want* to and hope I'm not scarin' you off. But if you don't anymore, I promise I won't fuss or anything." Utterly agonized, she wound down, then whispered desperately, "I love you."

She was so uncertain because she didn't know he felt. But then, *he* didn't know how he felt.

"I swear," she added, "I wouldn't tease and make you think… I wouldn't lead you on only to throw out this emotional baggage and then bail on you. Noel told me—"

He latched onto that. "Noel?"

She nodded fast, her hands still holding on to him as if she feared he might run screaming away from her.

*Because she loved him.*

"Noel told me not to play Amber's games. He said—"

More confusing by the moment. Adam put a finger to her mouth and shook his head. He needed a second. Or maybe a day.

He needed *her*.

"What does my busy-body cousin have to do with this?"

Issy shied away. "I, um…"

"Isabella?"

Hearing him use her full name, she lifted her chin. "I told her I loved you. That is, she offered to fix me up with some different guys and I told her it was *you* I wanted, that it was because of you I hadn't been datin' and…" She trailed off, becoming subdued once more. "Stuff."

"Stuff," he repeated stupidly. "What *stuff*?"

She shrugged. "Sex stuff."

Poleaxed, Adam struggled to catch up. So she'd been celibate… "Because you want me?"

She nodded, then inhaled again.

And this time it was Adam bracing.

"I want you so much, Adam." Her small hand moved over his chest, then up his shoulder to the back of his neck. Gaze pleading, she whispered, "Today. *Right now*. Okay? Please?"

He had no idea if he should be relieved or not. "I want you, too."

Her smile came, then went. "But…and this is the tricky part."

Oh good. A *tricky* part. He worked his jaw. "Let's hear it."

"If you're not…if you don't have feelins for me, too, then…" She winced. "It should probably just be this one time."

It took a second for that to sink in. "One time…" sounded completely inadequate.

Staring up at him, Issy nodded. "One time to relieve the itch, or satisfy your curiosity or whatever it is you're feelin' for me." Her gaze moved over him, hopeful, and damn but he saw the love.

*For him*.

"Amber told me you needed a nudge. She said you were so determined on bein' a bachelor that you might not even recognize your own feelings. So I went along with her game."

"Game?"

She bit her lips and nodded. "To give you that nudge."

"By flaunting other possible guys in front of me?"

She winced, guilt stealing her gaze away so that she stared at the lake. "See, that was the plan at first. But before I could even give it a go, you approached me at the carnival and I wasn't interested in that game anymore." Her gaze returned to his face. "Only Amber didn't know that, so she carried on. And between us, everything seemed to happen at once."

Because he'd already been changing—without Amber's damned intrusion. *When he saw his cousin again—*

"If you feel more for me," Issy said quietly, drawing him back around, "then I'm here. I'm yours."

His heart leapt at that, then started hammering. *I'm yours.* Elation coursed through him, ramping up his possessiveness, further sharpening his need, though how that was possible he didn't know. He'd already wanted her more than any other woman, but now... what he felt wasn't even in the same stratosphere of anything familiar.

"If that's not what you want," she continued, her expression watchful, wary. "If you don't feel that way about me, then please, for my sake, let's make it only once."

The *once* being... "You mean this time? Here and now?"

She nodded. "*Just* this time, if all you want is sex."

Still feeling a little numb and far too slow, Adam asked, "Do I have time to think about it?"

She gave a nearly hysterical laugh, but quickly cut it off with a hand over her mouth. Encouraged that he was still here, talking about it, she nodded fast. "Yes, of course." She stroked her hand down his chest. "We could go up to my house now and..."

He cupped her face. "Sate our curiosity?"

"Yes. And you can think about it then, and later, and...take all the time you need."

Never in his life had he felt so lost in confusion. Or

so turned on. It wasn't just the lust churning through his bloodstream, leaving him almost lightheaded.

His chest felt...full.

With emotion.

He wasn't yet sure if that emotion was fear, or relief, or...what the hell it might be. There was just too damned much of it. So much, he thought he might choke on it.

He needed to act, so he did. Stepping to the boat, he retrieved his wallet, jammed it into his pocket, and bounded back out to the dock where he scooped her up and damn near ran up the hill to her house.

"Your sunglasses!" she said. "They're still on the wall—"

Adam kissed her. He didn't care about his sunglasses. He didn't care about his cousin's warped games. He wouldn't have cared about his wallet...except that's where he kept an emergency condom, thank God.

He wanted Issy. He had her in his arms.

Curiosity, hell. His need was so powerful, it felt like a ticking time bomb.

## CHAPTER EIGHT

LUCKILY THE BACKDOOR of her house wasn't locked up, because Adam didn't want to put her down. Practically jogging, he raced to the small patio, adjusted her so he could slide the door open, and found himself in her kitchen. His heart thundered. "Which way?"

Squeezing him, her face against his neck, Issy said breathlessly, "Down the hall, last room to the right."

He passed other rooms, but didn't care. As he rushed into her bedroom, he temporarily stalled.

It was…pretty. Girly, even. Braided rugs covered the hardwood floor. White and sky blue gauzy curtains coordinated with a patchwork quilt done in wildflower patterns.

Another facet to her personality.

Then he forgot about her room and lowered her to her feet.

"I'm wet," she said.

"Good to know." Reaching around her, he untied the bra top to her suit.

Issy held it in place. "No, I mean my hair and—"

He kissed her, *devoured* her, until she forgot about everything but him. Her arms came around his neck and he tossed the wet top aside, then slid his hands into her bottoms.

"Oh." When he went to his knees, taking the bottoms with him, Issy braced her hands on his shoulders.

Breathing hard, Adam sat back on his heels and gazed at her naked body. Long ropes of wet hair trailed around her pale breasts, leading his attention to the dip of her narrow waist and slight curve to her belly, then down the length of her slender thighs. Damn, she was perfect.

Perfect for him.

Pulling her to him, he put a gentle love bite to her ribs, then her belly...and her inner thigh.

He rubbed his nose over her skin, drinking in her scent, filling his head with the aroused, rich, sun-warmed female fragrance. "God," he groaned, turning the soft bites to open-mouthed kisses, tasting her, wanting to eat her up.

"Adam." Tenderly, she coasted her fingers through his hair. "Come up here to me."

Instead he tumbled her onto the bed, then settled over her. Long lashes half lowered in a heavy, aroused expression of excitement. "Stay just like this," he told her. "Promise me."

She nodded.

Levering up and off her, Adam dug in his back pocket, removed his wallet and opened it to find the lone condom tucked away.

"Aren't you resourceful," Issy teased.

"I don't take chances." Except that here, with her, he was. *I love you.* Her words kept playing in his head, over and over and each damn time it made his muscles tighter.

And his dick harder.

He needed to be inside her—but first he needed her

back to the breaking point, gasping, squeezing him, moving against him...

Jesus. Holding the condom packet in his teeth, Adam looked at her while shucking off his shorts.

Her lips parted and she rose to one elbow.

"Ah-ah," Adam told her after tearing open the foil packet. "You promised not to move." He rolled on the rubber and came down over her again. "I like you just like this."

Breathing harder, she nodded. "I like this too." One of her legs hooked over his and she coasted her foot up the back of his calf, then his thigh, until she could wrap her leg around him. "You feel so good."

He held both her breasts, bringing them together and bending to kiss her nipples, to lick at her, suck on her—make her urgent again.

She got there pretty quickly.

"Adam." Arching her back and better offering up her breasts, she held his head to her.

"I want you to come for me."

"Yes." She tried to move under him, probably hoping to hurry him along.

Wasn't going to happen.

Didn't matter that he went nuts with wanting her, he needed to know it was good for her—and that meant letting her go first.

"Take it easy."

"I've been wantin' you too long."

He started to say, *Me too.* But was that true? At the moment, it felt like he'd been waiting a lifetime for her. He said instead, "Shh..." and kissed his way down her body.

Issy squirmed, gasped, purred with each small nibble, leisurely lick, or soft suck.

Slipping off the side of the bed, he caught her hips, pulled her to the edge, and arranged her legs over his shoulders.

"Adam?"

The excited, rasping way she said his name turned him on even more. He nibbled his way from her inner knee to the top of her thigh, parted her gently with his fingers, and covered her with his mouth.

"Oh...*wow*." Her tender thighs closed reflexively against his jaws as Adam moved his tongue over her, in her, then up to her small, swollen clitoris.

As he drew on her, she cried out, her hips lifting. He splayed one hand over her belly to hold her still and lifted the other to her breast, teasing her nipple.

She tasted so good and smelled even better and Adam knew he could spend an hour eating her. But far too soon she quickened, her thighs tensing, her belly clenching, hands fisted in the quilt and—

She cried out, at first high, then low and raw as her body squirmed and the pleasure drained her.

The second she went lax, while she was still gasping, Adam rose over her, pressed one leg wider, and sank into her with a vibrating groan. He wouldn't last, knew it, hated it, but already a hot rush of release stole his resolve and his senses.

Limply, Issy hugged him, her lips moving over his shoulder as his hips pounded against her. He was almost gone when he felt her tightening around him again. He squeezed his eyes and clenched his teeth and concentrated, holding off his own release, holding,

holding—until she broke. Then he lifted up to see her, his gaze locked on hers, and finally he let himself go.

AT SOME POINT Adam had turned to his back and brought Isabella with him. She rested atop him, her cheek to his chest, her body utterly lax.

Every so often Adam petted her, or kissed her shoulder or temple, occasionally fondling her backside.

She sighed and knew nothing could ever be more perfect.

*Unless he loved her.*

After waiting a half hour, the silence started to get to her. She came up to her elbows and found Adam wide awake, watching her with dark eyes and a disturbing intensity.

"Hey," she said, suddenly feeling shy.

He tucked back her hair. "Hey, yourself."

"That was…" Seriously, she had no words.

"Yeah." Using both hands he cupped her face and brought her down for a gentle kiss. "Very much so."

So he'd felt it too? Nice.

Hopefully he'd want to do it again, but she just didn't know. "Did you think about…you know?" She toyed with his chest hair and dared a quick peek at him. "What I said."

With deep concentration, he traced her mouth with one fingertip. "Thought about it, thinking about it, will think about it a lot more, I'm sure."

What did that mean?

He continued to touch her, lifting one of her hands so he could kiss each fingertip.

Because she had no idea what they were doing, Isabella said, "Tomorrow I'll go get the cat."

"Mmm." He kissed her wrist. "Want me to go with you?"

Did that mean..? If he offered to spend more time with her...was that an agreement of sorts to give a relationship a chance? She studied his expression, but other than looking sated, and tender and somehow cocky, she couldn't tell what he thought or felt.

"So..."

He smiled. "So?"

Okay, now her temper was starting to prickle. "Not to pressure you, but..?"

When his brows pinched, she quickly retrenched and said, "Never mind. Surprise me."

He turned her beneath him, stared at her, then took her mouth in a long, deep kiss. By small degrees, he lifted away and smiled down at her. "How about I call you in the morning?"

After that kiss, and with the feel of his big, firm body over hers, it took her a second to get her thoughts together. "Sure. That'd be great." Playing it cool, she shrugged. "If that's what you want."

His gaze dropped to her mouth. "I want you."

She reminded him, "You've had me."

"I want you again."

Her breath caught. "You mean...now?"

"Yeah, but I only had the one rubber."

Damn. "I should've bought some."

That made him grin again. "How about I bring more with me tomorrow?"

Her throat went tight. Trying to be firm, to stick with what she knew would be best, Isabella said, "I'd like that."

"Good." He bent to nibble on her shoulder, and honestly, the way the man nibbled got her very heated, very quickly.

"Adam, remember, I told you—"

"I know." He gathered her close, his arms framing her head, his mouth pressing a kiss to her forehead, the bridge of her nose, and then her chin. "I'll always be honest with you, Issy."

Oh no. She wasn't sure she wanted his bald honesty. She swallowed, nodded, and said warily, "Okay."

"I want more with you. This one time, stupendous as it might have been, wasn't near enough. Tomorrow won't be enough, either. But I don't know what will be enough. A lot happened, and it happened fast."

She understood that. "You noticin' me, and acting on it, and—"

He shook his head. "I've always noticed you, you need to know that. But until yesterday you always seemed real untouchable. I'm not sure what was different, but when I saw you at the carnival, sitting on that quilt with your shoes off—"

She laughed. "So nekkid feet did it for ya, huh?"

"It wasn't just the 'nekkid' feet," he teased, mimicking her accent. "You flirted with me. You went from mere politeness to teasing and giving off a vibe—"

"I have a vibe?" She loved the sound of that.

"A very sexy vibe."

"Huh." This after-sex chitchat was pretty darned interesting. A woman could learn all sorts of things. "Amber coached me. She told me to—"

"Hush." Pressing a finger to her lips, Adam interrupted her. "I can't talk about my cousin while lying naked on you, thinking the things I'm thinking. The two just don't mix."

Excitement bubbled up. "What're you thinkin'?"

"Raunchy things," he whispered. "Sweet things. Nasty, hot, sexual and tantalizing things."

Her toes curled, and she asked, "About me?"

"Don't say it like that surprises you." He laughed and kissed her again, then sat up. "You're gorgeous, especially like this."

"Nekkid."

"Yeah."

She laughed, too. So much happiness cocooned her, she wanted to get up and dance.

But she'd definitely get dressed before she did anything like that.

Adam Sommerville, Buckhorn's most sought after bachelor, was in her bed. They'd made love—wonderful, hot, mind-blowing sex—and now she got to look at his wide, bare back while he sat on the side of her bed teasing her.

Feeling daring, she asked, "Do you need to leave?"

His gaze locked on hers. "Not unless you want me to."

Heck no. If she could have her way, he'd never budge. "Gettin' hungry?" she asked. "I could cook."

"I don't want you to go to any trouble. We could order pizza or something."

Isabella wrinkled her nose. "I like to cook."

"If you're sure, then yes, I'm starved." As if he'd been doing so for years, he idly cupped her breast. "How about we compromise and I'll grill? We can sit out back and enjoy the sunset."

Ohhh. So romantic. "I'd love that."

He stood and stretched.

And in the process he almost turned her into a puddle of excited hormones.

So far, this was all going so well.

Isabella couldn't wait to share with Amber. Not only did she count Amber as a friend and confidante, but she needed to let her know that things had definitely changed.

Before Amber introduced her to any other men, Isabella wanted to put all her concentration on making things work with Adam.

At the moment, that was about all she could handle.

## *CHAPTER NINE*

SHE NAMED THE cat Cupid. Seemed appropriate to Adam, considering the cat had played a hand in helping him get closer to Issy. All week he watched her with Cupid, and it brought back memories of other things.

She bought the cat toys, and he thought of the times he'd seen her gift books to underprivileged students.

She groomed Cupid, and he thought of the time he'd walked into the library and found her fixing a girl's hair when one of her braids had come undone. When she'd finished, that braid looked better than the other, so she'd redone the second one also, neatly tying ribbons to the ends of both. The girl had given her a shy smile, a fast hug, then taken the book Issy offered and went off to read.

He could still recall how he'd stood there, watching Issy as she smiled after the child, a look of tenderness in her eyes. No one would ever call her *just* a librarian, because she was so much more. Librarian, fighter for the underdog, motivated giver, caring supervisor, and sexy manipulator... Isabella Presley was a complex, complicated, fascinating woman with an enormous capacity for love.

That day in the school library, she'd been wearing a below-the-knee black pencil skirt with flats and a tucked-in white blouse, her hair in a twist at the back of her neck. He'd teased himself with the thought of kissing her nape, then stripping her out of those sedate clothes.

He'd approached her, as he often had, but as usual she'd been all business without a single flirting note in her voice. Now, of course, he realized it was her professionalism and her awareness of students nearby that had kept her from engaging in anything other than respectful small talk.

One memory always led to another, and he realized...he'd been a fool. Always, in so many different ways, Issy had shown herself to be very special. He should have been more attuned to his own attraction and stated his interest instead of expecting her to act first.

Maybe he was too damned used to women chasing him.

Issy would never chase—except she had come up with a pretty creative way to get his attention...with the help of his meddling cousin.

And thinking of Amber, he knew he needed to clue her in on his and Issy's new relationship, especially after he pulled up to her house and for the third day in a row, found other men already there.

Issy stood on the porch, dressed casually in a T-shirt and shorts and looking sexier than ever with her dark red hair loose. By her animated face and hand gestures, Adam knew she was making her excuses, but the guys kept grinning and trying to persuade her otherwise.

Deciding to lend a hand, he slammed his door—and drew all their attention. He smiled as he made his way toward them.

"Adam," Issy said, sounding suddenly breathless. "You're early."

"I finished up sooner than I thought." He ignored Ken and Gary, stepped past them, scooped Issy in for a passionate kiss, and while she was preoccupied with that, he stepped them both inside and kicked the door shut. Ending the kiss with reluctance, he looked down at Issy's closed eyes and parted lips and appreciated the heavier way she breathed. "They'll leave now," he assured her.

Her heavy eyelids lifted. "Who?"

Ah, nice that the chemistry was so strong for both of them. "The yahoos on your porch."

"My porch," she repeated, and a second later her eyes flared. "The men!" She pushed Adam aside, opened the door and...

Damn, they both still stood there.

"I am *so* sorry," Issy said. She frowned at Adam to ensure they all knew where she placed the blame.

Ken grinned at her. "No problem."

Rubbing the smile off his mouth, Gary said, "Say yes, and we can get out of your way."

Aggressive confusion had Adam crossing his arms and mean-mugging both men.

"Adam," Issy said, "Ken and Gary are here about a game-day fundraiser."

"We have it on good authority that she's a shark at horseshoes." Ken gave her a sappy smile. "We need her on our team."

"I'm really not," Issy insisted. "I keep telling you—"

"Turly already told us." Gary slanted a look at Adam. "He said she's *real* good."

"So we *need* you," Ken repeated.

And damn it, Adam just knew they were wording their pleas in a way to annoy him.

"The fundraiser isn't for another month." He and his family always participated. Several different sports and games were set up and throughout the day fellow citizens competed for a fee. Whoever won each sport got to designate which local non-profit received the funds.

"Got to grab her up quick," Ken said, "before someone else does."

"If we win," Gary added, "the money will go to the town library."

Of all the underhanded tricks! Gary and Ken usually put their winnings toward the lake, adding benches for sitting, or trees along the shoreline to help draw carp.

The bait worked though, and Issy perked up. "Really? Oh, that's wonderful."

Fast, before he got pushed aside, Adam said, "I wanted you on my team—for horseshoes and volleyball. I figured we'd divide our wins with one going to the library, and the other to help with the feral cat population."

Even more enthused, she said, "Oh, Adam, that would be *perfect*!"

Adam reeled her on in, saying, "We could maybe try our hands at softball, too, if you're interested. Think of all the money we could donate if we won all three."

She grabbed him for a tight hug. Over her head, Adam let Gary and Ken see his smug satisfaction.

Because they were going out to dinner, where Adam could show the whole town that they were a couple, Issy said her goodbyes to the others and hurried inside for her purse.

Taking advantage of the moment, Adam propped a shoulder against the doorjamb and tried to make a point. "I'm glad to know you were only here to ask her to compete."

Gary cocked a brow. "First I asked her out, and when she said no to that, I moved on to the games."

Damn it. Provoked, Adam slowly straightened.

"Same here," Ken said, drawing Adam's frown his way. "I figured when I pulled up and heard her refusing Gary, I might have a chance. But I struck out, too."

Of all the... Thumb to his chest, Adam stated, "Neither of you has a chance because she's with *me*."

"Sure, sure." Clapping him on the shoulder, Ken turned to go. "Good luck convincing everyone else."

"Just so you know," Gary added, "I've been after her for a long time."

Adam ground his teeth. "Now you can stop."

"Maybe. Think I'll wait and see how it works out with you first." He saluted Adam and left to catch up with Ken.

Adam was still stewing when he felt a brush against his legs and looked down to find Cupid staring after the men. Adam knew if he went to pick up the cat, she'd shy away.

She was still pretty timid with most people. He could pet her with an outstretched arm, but she wasn't keen on being held. Yet. He could force the issue, but would rather wait.

Between him, Issy, and his dad, Cupid was warming up. All she needed was plenty of love and patience. Issy had a wealth of both. "You should learn to be a guard cat. Keep all those other rats away."

Cupid meowed, then darted in to find Issy.

He and the cat had something in common.

They were both crazy about Isabella Presley.

Every Day For the rest of the week, Adam finished his day by showing up at Isabella's. They'd have dinner, make love, then sleep curled together.

The situation would have been perfect, except that far too often when he got to her place, he found other guys there. Oh, they had a variety of reasons for visiting that on the surface sounded innocent enough.

But he wasn't buying it.

Now that Issy was on the market, it seemed every bachelor in Buckhorn wanted to try his chances with her.

It got to where his routine included thinking about Issy when he wasn't with her, finally getting to her only to have to chase off the competition, and then spending the rest of his time trying to ensure she wasn't interested in other guys.

She helped by repeatedly stating her love. He'd gotten used to that, to hearing those three small but awesome words from her. Even though he hadn't yet said them back, he knew the truth.

He loved being with her, loved touching her, talking to her—and especially loved sex with her. He couldn't imagine a woman more compatible with him, and didn't even want to imagine himself with anyone else.

Isabella was it for him.

The only reason he hesitated to state his feelings was because it almost felt forced. Not by Isabella, but by his damned cousin who, he felt sure, was the one repeatedly tossing guys at her. Amber would probably do it to both annoy him and prod him toward declarations. But he wanted Issy to know he wasn't coerced in any way, to understand that he'd already been interested long before they ramped up things at the carnival. Kissing her had sealed the deal. Getting close to her had completely stolen his heart.

Given a little time, he could show her how much he cared, instead of merely telling her. But time didn't seem to be on his side.

Within an hour of them getting to the family picnic on Sunday, two local guys who'd showed up with Garrett began to flirt with her. Cupid wasn't happy about being in a carrier, and she especially didn't like the guys talking so loud.

They'd brought her along because Jordan wanted to check her over again. His uncle often did vet checks of the family pets at big gatherings. Eventually Cupid would come to enjoy all the attention, but for now, there'd be a quiet place in the house for her during their visit.

Using the cat as an excuse, Adam pointed the pushy guys in the direction of his Uncle Gabe's daughters, Briana, April and Kady. For sure, those three flirts would keep them occupied.

He glared at Garrett, who just grinned and hugged Zoey closer. "Problem, Adam?"

"No." Not since he got the guys to move on. If he had his way, he'd end the date-parade today. He said to Issy, "Cupid would probably like to get out of this carrier, and I'm betting Garrett and Zoey would love to meet her."

Garrett, who'd started to move toward one of the coolers for a beer, froze. He glanced at Adam, cocked a brow, and then proved himself loyal by saying, "Yeah, that'd be great. But why don't we all go inside first, in case Cupid freaks out?"

Issy, who'd been cooing to the cat, smiled at Garrett. "She's really very sweet—"

A feral snarl emerged.

Taking the carrier from Issy, Garrett soothed both the cat and her by saying, "Poor baby isn't liking all the commotion. Let's take her in." Winking at Adam, he added, "You can go ahead and have that talk with Amber. We'll be fine."

Zoey laughed. "My money's on Amber." She hooked her arm through Isabella's and got them moving.

"I'll be right back," Adam called after them.

Always happy to brag about her pet, Isabella nodded and off she went with his bemused cousin Garrett, and Zoey, who was always enthusiastic about everything.

It required only a short search before Adam located Amber in the kitchen, stealing a kiss from Noel Poet.

"Ahem," he said loudly.

Noel ignored him, but Amber jumped away guiltily. "Adam. Hey, you're here. What's up?"

Rolling his eyes, Noel said, "Judging by the look on his face, your goose is cooked, that's what."

"I don't know what you—"

Noel kissed her again, short and sweet. "I'll give you two some privacy."

"Traitor," Amber grumbled, then she pasted on a smile. "Adam. You do look a little grouchy. Everything going okay?"

Knowing Issy was in the house and could show up at any minute, Adam crowded close to whisper, "I thought you loved me."

She grinned. "I do. Very much."

"Then quit with the interfering."

On a feigned gasp of indignation, she said, "I *assist*. There's a difference."

"Your brand of assistance is about to make me insane."

Going serious, she said, "Hey, I called them off."

"Right." If that was true, she must not have been very convincing.

"I did," she insisted.

"When?"

"Soon as you told me you were involved, that day at her house." She shrugged. "I guess now that they've made note of her, they're free agents. Not my doing. Just men going after what they want."

"Issy?"

She patted Adam's shoulder. "You have to admit, the woman is a catch."

"Of course she is. She's beautiful and smart and sweet."

"Sexy, too?" Amber asked.

"Smokin' hot." He let out a breath. If it wasn't Amber encouraging the men, he needed to think of a way to *discourage* them.

"She's good with kids, too."

"You don't have to tell me." Adam rubbed the back of his neck. "She's incredible with them. Understanding and genuinely caring. One day, she'll make a terrific mother."

Both brows up, Amber asked, "With you as the father?"

"That's the plan, if I can—"

Behind him, Issy gasped.

Adam jerked around, and there she stood, Cupid cuddled in her arms, her eyes wide with astonishment.

Zoey and Garrett grinned behind her.

Damn it. Of all the ways he'd considered declaring himself, this wasn't one of them. "Hey."

She blinked those big blue eyes at him. "Hey."

Amber sighed. "I love it when a plan comes together." She bestowed an approving smile on each of them, gathered up Garrett and Zoey, and exited the kitchen.

For once, Adam appreciated her efforts. At least now he and Issy had some privacy.

He closed the distance between them, brushed his knuckles along her jaw, and asked, "What do you think?"

Face going pink, she whispered, "About?"

"Having babies with me. Not just yet, but someday. After we're married, of course."

For one heart-stopping moment, her bottom lip trembled. "I guess that depends." After a deep breath, she asked, "Do you love me?"

"Very, very much."

All the starch left her, and she even lightly punched him. "Why didn't you tell me?"

"I didn't want you to think it was Amber's idea. I know how she manipulates things."

"She does?"

How could Issy be unaware of that? "She told you not to tell me how you felt, right?"

Warily, Issy nodded. "Yes."

To let her know it was okay, Adam kissed her forehead. "Amber didn't want me to get too cocky about things." Without making an issue of it, he led her out of the kitchen and down the hall. He needed to ensure they'd have a few minutes alone, and he wanted to hold her—which meant getting her to an enclosed room where she could put down Cupid. "But after you gave me the cold shoulder so many times, there wasn't much chance of that happening."

"I *never*."

"Yeah, honey, you did."

Under her breath, she grumbled, "Well, how's a woman to know what you're thinkin'?"

"Usually if I talked to a woman, she'd chat back, flirt a little, open the door to more. But you were always all business and I guess I didn't want to get shot down."

"I wouldn't have," she said gently. "And I hesitated to be bolder with you for the same reason. You're Buckhorn's most wanted bachelor, and I'm just—"

"Amazing." Pausing in the hallway, he kissed her. "Wonderful." Another kiss. "And mine."

Leaning into him, she sighed. "Yes." Then she shook her head and laughed. "Yes to being yours. I don't know about the rest."

"You can take my word on it." So much time they'd wasted. Sometimes his cousin was a genius—not that he'd ever admit it to her. "Amber also told me you were a little wild," he teased.

"*Wild?*" Face hotter now, Issy didn't hesitate when he led her into an empty bedroom and closed the door. "That's ridiculous."

Not really. He had no idea how Amber had known, but when it came to sex—or at least, sex with him—Isabella was open, free, and totally uninhibited.

In other words, *perfect*.

But then, she was pretty much perfect in everything she did, whether it was running a middle school library, caring for kids in need, charming the masses, or making him insane with lust. "I assume Amber told me that to get me intrigued. Thing is, I was always intrigued. You need to know that."

Sitting on the side of the bed, Issy released a wiggling Cupid who wanted to sniff the room. Without the cat to hold, she laced her fingers together. "You hid it well."

"No, honey, you're just not great at picking up the signals. Too many times, I was all but panting for you."

"No," she said with fascinated disbelief.

Adam had no problem reassuring her. "Yup. But now that we're together, it doesn't matter."

"Because you love me?" She said it as if she couldn't quite bend her brain around it.

That was his fault. In trying to prove a point with Amber, he'd left Isabella uncertain.

"How could I not?" he asked. "Everything about you has always drawn me, but with my cousin putting her nose into things, we've now been able to talk in a more..." He fumbled for the right word.

"Intimate way?"

"Yes." He grinned, thinking of all the ways they'd been intimate. "That." Sitting beside her, Adam took her worried hands and held them. "Not for a second do I want you to think Amber talked me into anything. I've always wanted you, Issy, always liked you and been drawn to you. If you'd opened up more a year ago, we'd probably be married by now."

Her eyes went round.

It wasn't a quite a proposal, but more like a declaration of intent.

"We have time," he told her. "Time to do everything you want, time for me to show you how much I care, time to just enjoy being together before we start rushing into new plans." He didn't want her to feel pressured.

Cupid wound around their legs, leaving her long tail out until she'd formed a furry shackle.

Carefully, so he wouldn't spook her, Adam scooped her up and into Issy's lap. "What do you say we start by getting engaged? That way everyone will know you're not available. We can take our time figuring out everything else."

She didn't even blink. "I'd like that."

Smiling, he said, "We can pick out rings whenever you want."

Nodding hard, she gasped, "Okay."

Adam had to kiss her, so he did. As usual, she tasted so good, stirred him on so many levels, that he got carried away. Things might have gotten inappropriate, given they were in his uncle's house, except that Cupid's tail hit him in the chin, reminding him of the here and now.

He leaned away with a grin. "I want everyone to know you're taken."

Staring at his mouth, she whispered, "Long as they know you're taken, too."

"I'll be telling it to everyone who'll listen." And definitely to anyone male who came sniffing around Issy.

"I love you," she whispered.

Adam cupped her face, his heart full. "I love you, too."

A tap sounded at the door, and Amber gave a loud, "Ahem."

Adam groaned. "What now?"

"Everyone's gathered to eat if you two want to make any—hint, hint—announcements."

Adam stood and opened the door. "It's uncanny how you do that."

Beaming, she bragged, "I have my skills."

Issy appeared at his side, leaning into him while holding Cupid. "Do your skills include ropin' in Noel Poet?"

Amber frowned. "I'm working on it."

From behind her, Noel said, "Good to know."

Aghast, Amber went still, then red in the face before slowly pivoting to face Noel. "It's rude to sneak up on people."

"That's never stopped you."

Adam enjoyed seeing his cousin in the hot seat for once.

Issy broke the growing tension with a happy laugh. "Neither of you are showin' Amber the appreciation she deserves." Issy smiled up at him. "Adam and I are gettin' engaged, and I couldn't be happier!"

"And before your head gets any bigger," Adam said to Amber, "you only played the *smallest* of roles in it."

"Small, but integral," Amber countered, grabbing them both for hugs. "Now let's go make that announcement!"

Noel caught her arm before she could take a single step away. "Since you already know what's going on, you don't need to be there." Ignoring her protests, he urged her into the room they'd just vacated, and right before he closed the door, he said to Adam, "Congrats to you both."

Surprised, Adam stared at the closed door, and slowly smiled.

"She deserves to be happy," Issy whispered.

They both heard Amber say, "Now wait just a—" Then her voice faded into a soft hum.

"She does," Adam agreed. "I'd say Noel has her well on her way." Putting a hand to the small of Issy's back, he led her out front. The sooner everyone knew Isabella's changed circumstances, the sooner he could relax. And then they could get started on their future.

\* \* \* \* \*

*The Buckhorn Brothers—hot, protective, and oh-so-alpha...especially around the women they love.*

*Don't miss any of the Buckhorn series, Available now from Lori Foster and HQN Books!*

*BUCKHORN BEGINNINGS*
*(featuring Sawyer and Morgan)*

*FOREVER BUCKHORN*
*(featuring Gabe and Jordan)*

*THE BUCKHORN LEGACY*
*(featuring Casey)*

*BUCKHORN EVER AFTER*
*(Shohn and Nadine's story)*

*BACK TO BUCKHORN*
*(Garrett and Zoey's story)*

*A BUCKHORN SUMMER*
*(Lisa and Gray's story)*

# A
# BUCKHORN
## SUMMER

# *CHAPTER ONE*

ONE MONTH AGO TODAY, she'd awakened disoriented in a posh hotel in Chicago. Exhausted. Tired of travel.

Lonely.

For the longest time she'd stared at the ceiling, getting her bearings and knowing she needed a break. Her stomach had burned from too much stress. Her neck hurt from the small, flat pillow.

Lisa Sommerville had known instinctively that she needed a change, so she'd gotten up, dressed, gone down to the bar and...

"Lighten up," her cousin Shohn said from behind her as he turned the small outboard motor on the fishing boat, steering around a sunken log and aiming toward the marina where they'd gas up and grab bait. "You'll have fun. Guaranteed."

On the seat in front of her, the bright morning sunlight making a halo of his fair hair, her brother, Adam, grinned. "No thinking about work, remember? If we catch you drifting off, Dad gave us permission to drop you in the lake."

Lisa looked over the side of the boat. The water was green and cool and this early in the day, fairly smooth. "I wasn't."

"Fibber," Adam said.

"That's all you think about," Shohn agreed. "But not today."

She didn't bother to correct them, to explain that her thoughts had been on her very out-of-character behavior from a month ago. On the sizzling night she'd had. On the fantasy that had come to life and still, every other minute, replayed in her mind.

"Lisa," Adam warned, again mistaking her quiet.

She looked up at the blinding sunrise splashing colors across a cloudless sky. "I'll probably take a dip on my own later." She slanted a look at her brother. "On my own, without your help, after I've put on my suit."

"You could swim in that," Shohn said, indicating her outfit of shorts and a blue T-shirt.

She turned her narrowed gaze on him, prompting him to grin like the sinner she knew him to be. They all three had dark eyes, but the similarities ended there. She was medium height, with medium-length honey-blond hair and a medium figure. Shohn and Adam both topped six feet. Adam's hair was far fairer than hers, and Shohn's was inky black.

Both men lived and worked in Buckhorn, Shohn as a park ranger, Adam as a gym teacher.

She loved Buckhorn as well, but until that fateful night in Chicago, she'd also loved traveling the country, working 24-7, earning her barracuda rep in the business world.

Icy water hit her legs, making her gasp.

"Concentrate," Shohn said, flicking his now wet fingers at her face, "or I'll grab a bucketful of water instead of just a handful."

"I was concentrating!" She brushed water droplets off her heated thighs.

"On *fun*," Adam stressed. "Not work."

Because they'd just reached the dock, Lisa didn't reply. Without waiting for the boat to steady, she stood and leaped out, a rope in hand, and secured the front of the small boat to a cleat.

Shohn did the same to the back. Adam, holding their bait bucket, hauled himself out behind her.

Every woman around stared. Always. Her cousin and brother had that effect wherever they went. Between them, she felt insubstantial, inadequate, even bland.

Which in part explained why she'd glommed onto business. In a family full of prime physical specimens, male and female alike, she was just so-so.

Except for when it came to brains and drive. Then she excelled.

Or used to. Now she considered changing it all. She could join her family in the slower, easier life of Buckhorn County, Kentucky. Doing what, she didn't yet know.

Fishing today. But tomorrow? She was not an idle person.

"We lost her again."

Sure, she needed to slow down. Her health and her very recent aberrant behavior proved she needed that change. No one in her family yet knew of her tension, her migraines, her sleepless nights.

Only that one man, a man she'd never see again—

She screeched when Shohn scooped her up and headed to the side of the dock. "Ohmigod, don't you dare!"

"You need to be dunked."

Knotting one hand in his dark hair, the other in his

worn T-shirt, she growled, "Try it and you're going in with me. Or at least your hair is." She gave a tug to prove her point.

Wincing, laughing, Shohn said, "I'll jump us both in."

"No!" Okay, sure, her lake clothes, as she called them, wouldn't be harmed, but she'd braided her hair and didn't want it soaked. "Seriously," she said more calmly. *"No."*

Standing beside them, Adam crossed his arms over his bare chest. "Then no more brooding over business."

Lisa blew out a huff of breath. "If you must know, I wasn't."

"Bull."

"I was thinking of...a guy." *There*, she thought. *Chew on that.*

Both men laughed.

*Laughed.*

Was it so unheard of for her to be socially interested and interesting? Admitting the pathetic truth, she knew that yes, it was. At thirty, she'd never had a single serious romantic relationship.

She'd had some dates. She'd had some sex.

She'd had that one amazing night that would forever leave her warm and wanting...for more, more, more.

But she'd never been involved. And damn it, that hurt.

Mouth tight and brows angled down, Lisa turned her face away.

The laughter died.

Shohn slowly lowered her to her feet, obliging her to release his hair.

Without a word, Adam slung an arm around her

shoulders and again got them heading along the dock to the gravel lot alongside the boat launch and then up the worn path to the small renovated structure that sold anything and everything boaters might need.

Hoping to clear the air, Lisa asked, "When did this change?" She remembered the structure being smaller, more weatherworn and utilitarian. Now it looked like a regular two-story house, complete with flowers planted around the exterior.

The double front doors, standing open, and the picnic tables placed all around the area made it clear the store remained, but otherwise it could have been any other home in Buckhorn.

"Rosemary sold the marina some years back to a married couple who did the additions. But they sold it a few weeks ago and retired to Arizona to be nearer to their grandkids. A new guy stepped right in and the place never closed, not even for a day. It was pretty seamless."

"Huh." So it had changed hands twice and she'd been unaware. Crazy how detached she'd been from her home. "I like the addition of a second level. Does the owner live here?"

"I dunno," Shohn said. "I've only met him a few times. He's friendly, but not real talkative, which I guess makes sense given he's a retired cop."

"You'll probably like him," Adam teased. "All the single ladies seem to."

Sure enough, as they stepped into the building, Lisa saw a trio of bikini-clad women huddled around the front counter and register, giggling in amped-up flirt mode.

She snorted. It was barely eight a.m., but the ladies

were already on the prowl. The new guy must be interesting. Then again, Buckhorn was such a small, intimate town that anyone new got plenty of attention.

Shohn headed for the live bait selection, Adam went to fill the cooler with drinks and she moseyed down an aisle to pick up sunscreen. As a kid, she'd kept a light tan. As a woman who'd spent most of her time traveling from one business meeting to the next, her skin rarely saw prolonged exposure to the sun.

She remembered fishing trips from her youth and knew the guys would keep her out for hours, maybe right through lunch. She grabbed the sunscreen and a straw hat.

Heading for the snacks, she turned, took two steps—and gasped.

So did the man standing in front of her.

The big, sinfully gorgeous man.

The man with the amazing bod and killer smile and devour-you sex drive.

The man from a month ago.

Her...*fantasy*.

GRAY NARROWED HIS eyes, but the vision didn't change. Big brown eyes locked on his. Those sweet, lush lips parted. Color filled her cheeks.

It was her, but an all-new version of her. A softer, sexier version, though how that was possible, he didn't know, because every night for a freaking month he'd remembered her as so damned sexy, he felt obsessed.

Neither of them spoke. Hell, he didn't know what to say.

*Let's go for round two* didn't seem appropriate.

Shohn Hudson and Adam Sommerville, cousins he'd met before, suddenly flanked her.

Cocking a brow, expression cautious, Shohn asked, "Problem?"

Yeah, about a hundred of them. Gray didn't know her name, didn't know why she was here, didn't know if she remembered him or was horrified at seeing him again or if, God willing, she'd like to get reacquainted.

Adam slipped his arm around her and, yeah, that was another problem. *Don't let her be married.* Or even involved. In any way.

"You're new," Gray finally said, regaining his voice, rough and low as it sounded. His interest must've been obvious given how both Adam and Shohn looked at her again, almost as if they'd never seen her before.

She cleared her throat, worked up a very bright, false smile, and stepped away from the two men with her hand extended. "Hello. I'm Lisa Sommerville. Adam's sister."

Related? Now that she'd said it, he could see it. She and Adam shared similar dark eyes. And if they were siblings, that'd make Hudson her cousin. Nice. Only related, not involved. He could work with that.

Tucking a small box of candy bars under his left arm, Gray accepted her hand and held on. "Gray Neely." Her hands were as small and soft as he remembered, her skin just as warm.

Her scent every bit as stirring.

She tugged, and he had no choice but to let her go. "Actually," she said, now a little breathless, "I'm local. *You're* the new one."

An accusation? "So you live here?" That'd be too

much of a coincidence—the first good luck he'd had in a year.

Her chin lifted. "Yes."

A slow smile growing, Adam looked between them. "Lisa's a shark, usually away wheeling and dealing with the big dawgs in business."

"She's settling back in for a spell, though," Shohn added.

"Maybe just the summer," she was quick to say.

Tipping his chin, Shohn asked, "You two know each other?"

Gray waited, and sure enough Lisa—pretty name—said too quickly, her voice a little high, *"No."*

Okay, he got that. Their time together wasn't really the sort you discussed with a brother or cousin.

"Not yet," Gray corrected, and watched her face go warm. He nodded at the hat she held. "Good idea. Going to be a scorcher today." And with that he continued on his way, restocking the candy bars on the shelf.

He heard whispering, curiosity from the guys, insistence from Lisa.

Damn, he really liked that name. It suited her.

Nice that he could now add it into the repeat fantasy that played in his head every other minute. That fantasy had been his recent salvation.

He'd met her on a desperate night during a time when nothing made sense and he hadn't known which way to turn. She'd been fighting her own demons and things had just...happened.

Scorching-hot things that had burned away his indecision and the pain of forced changes. For the remainder of the night they'd stayed tangled in erotic activity. He'd finally passed out, exhausted, sated, his brain blessedly clear of guilt and anger, her slim body held in his arms.

When he woke in the morning, she was gone.

But he'd tackled the day with a new outlook on life, and ended up in Buckhorn.

Now she was here, in the flesh, close at hand.

Glancing up, he saw the guys were teasing her and felt safe approaching again. "So how many of you are there in the area? Your family is large, right?"

Lisa moved on, pretending to consider the healthy snacks, but Adam and Shohn remained. "There's a bunch of us," Adam said, launching into a recitation of the many relatives, some of whom Gray had met, some he hadn't.

They were an impressive lot, and from what he could tell, they influenced a lot of the town. "I need to take notes to keep you all straight."

"Amber could help you with that. She's Garrett's sister."

"Met her," Gray said. Amber Hudson was beautiful, with dark hair and bright blue eyes and a smile that'd win over the darkest heart.

She also scared the pants off him. She had a bold manner and a controlling streak that kept him two cautious steps away. Not that two steps had been far enough. Within five minutes of meeting him she'd managed to get more info out of him than the rest of her relatives combined.

When Lisa looked up at him, he *felt* it. Her brows were slightly pinched, her expression uneasy. Because he'd met Amber?

Needing her to understand, to know his intent, he

stepped away from Shohn and Adam and approached her. "If you stay, what will you do?"

She breathed a little faster. "Do?"

Yeah, he liked the way her mind worked. Suppressing a smile, he said, "Jobwise."

"Oh."

Now she just looked flustered, and that was so different from the confident woman she'd been with him before that he had to feel his way carefully. "You are staying, right? That's what your cousin said."

She snatched up a granola bar, stared at it and put it back.

Indecisive? That, too, was different, but he didn't mind. He took a step closer, near enough to inhale the scent of her sun-warmed skin and hair. God, he remembered that scent, how it had mingled with his own when he'd moved over her, both of them naked.

"I'm not... I don't know yet." She licked her bottom lip, glanced past him to her relatives, saw they were chatting up some other customers and stared up at him with those big, soulful eyes.

"Shh," he whispered. "It's okay."

She swallowed.

"Far as anyone knows, or will ever know, this is the first time we've met." By sheer force of will he kept his hands to himself when what he really wanted, what he needed, was to touch her, to pull her small, soft body in against his—again. "You have my word."

She released a tense breath. "Thank you." As her cousin and brother drew near again, she added, "I haven't left my job. I mean, I tried to. I gave my four weeks' notice, but they countered with another promotion. I declined and they requested that I take the summer to think about it. So I guess I'm on a hiatus."

That night in the dim hotel bar in Chicago, she'd been teeming with restless energy. But here, now, he could see the remnants of exhaustion. Bone deep. The type of tiredness a person learned to live with.

He understood that, since he'd felt it himself many times. "They must appreciate you."

She nodded.

"What is it you do?"

Before she could answer, Shohn bragged on her. "She's a top-notch troubleshooter."

"Meaning she goes to businesses that are in trouble," Adam explained, "and analyzes their problems, then tells them the best way to be more efficient and profitable."

"She's been all over the country," Shohn added. "And sometimes out of the country."

"Guys..." Lisa protested.

"I think she should loaf for the summer." Adam nudged her. "Regroup and just play."

"She's earned it." Shohn added, "Problem is, Lisa doesn't do well with idle time. Never has."

"She'd go screaming nuts in under a week."

Giving them both a quelling frown, Lisa said to Gray, "I'm still considering my job prospects."

Prospects that could take her right back out of Buckhorn? Not if he could help it. "Could I make a suggestion?"

The guys were interested, but Lisa just looked appalled. Mind made up, he forged on. "I haven't been here that long and I'm still learning the ropes. If you're related to those two, then I assume you know everyone in town, and most of what there is to know about catering to vacationers."

She opened her mouth, but it was Shohn who said, "She does."

Adam added, "She's driven her fair share of boats, launched them, too, and even worked on them a few times with our uncle Gabe."

"Gabe, the handyman." Gray had met his daughters, all three of them. They were very pretty girls who flirted playfully. And they were all too young for him—not that he'd been interested anyway.

"When my uncle Jordan married Lisa's mom, she was still a kid," Shohn explained. "So she grew up around here. She knows everyone."

"Jordan, the vet?"

"Yup," Shohn said. "He has a real nice way with animals."

So one of the icons was her dad? "Got it."

"And," Adam continued, "being the overachiever she's always been, she's organized plenty of community activities with our uncle Morgan, back when he was sheriff and since he's been mayor."

Morgan, the big, badass protector. *Who the hell wasn't her relative?* Gray said only, "Met him, liked him."

Shohn said, "She's also—"

"Stop selling me!"

Her brother and cousin gaped at her. Grinning, Gray shook his head. "Amazing to me that either of you have hooked up. Not smooth, guys. Not smooth at all."

Adam scowled. "Now wait a minute. I wasn't—"

"It's okay," Gray assured him. Hell, he was already sold. It didn't require a pitch. Then to Lisa, he asked, "Why don't you come by tomorrow morning, say around six before I open, and we can discuss it?"

Her eyes widened. Both men stayed mute.

"The pay won't be what you're used to, but the work won't be, either. You want to enjoy the summer but also stay busy, right? I figure we can probably work out something fair. I'll be flexible on what hours you need to be here."

Amazingly, her eyes widened even more.

Cute as well as sexy. He could get lost in those dark eyes. In her slim throat, a pulse thrummed wildly. Her gaze remained fixed on his, and hell if he'd look away first. Didn't matter to him if they stood there all day.

Shohn nudged her, maybe a little harder than he meant to given that she stumbled.

Startled, she turned and smacked him. "What is *wrong* with you?"

"Me?" Shohn pointed at her. "You were the one gawking."

She flared. "I was not!"

Rolling his eyes, Adam said, "Yeah, you were."

Gray grinned. "You're all close, huh?"

"Very," Adam said with what sounded like a belated warning.

Having been a cop in a shit area rife with violent crime, Gray didn't pay a lot of attention to bluster. "What do you say, Lisa?" As an incentive, he added, "I promise to keep you busy without overworking you, and if you enjoy the lake, well, then, it could feel as much like an extended vacation as not."

Put on the spot, she finally nodded. "All right. Fine. I'll be here at six and we can discuss it."

"Not too early for you?"

Adam snorted. "She'll just be finishing up her jog."

Huh. So she liked to run? They had that in common. Gray wanted to know every little thing about her, but he could be patient. Maybe.

"If you're ready, I can ring you up."

Everyone followed him to the counter, and a minute after that he watched her go—his gaze glued to her small rounded butt in the short shorts. Damn. He remembered that sweet behind all too well, how it had fit in his hands, the tantalizing contrast of soft and firm.

With any luck at all, he'd be getting familiar again real soon.

## CHAPTER TWO

LUCKILY NO ONE was around when she untied the small fishing boat and pushed away from the dock. It took three pulls on the cord before she got the motor going, then she settled onto the hard wooden seat and started down the lake.

She could have used any of the boats; the family collectively had three inboard boats, two pontoons and a variety of rowboats and fishing boats. But this particular one was the quietest and she'd as soon not draw attention. She'd done enough of that already.

The sun had just started to rise from behind the hills, sending fingers of crimson and gold to cut through the lavender dawn and play across the calm surface of the lake. Taking it slow, Lisa watched a fish jump, saw a few birds diving, turned her face up to the warm, humid breeze.

She'd always loved the fast pace of her high-pressure job.

But she also loved the peace of the lake, and maybe it was past time to find a better balance between the two.

After showering off the sweat from her jog, she'd put on sunscreen and a touch of makeup. It hadn't been easy, dodging all the curious questions and over-the-top speculation from Adam and Shohn yesterday. They'd teased, harangued and outrageously guessed without ever once coming close to the truth.

That she'd had a sizzling-hot one-night stand with a total stranger who had now, by the fickle hand of fate, relocated to her hometown.

Shohn and Adam were both utter hedonists, open in their own sexual pursuits. But when it came to her—or any of the women in the family, really—they played deaf, dumb and blind, at least with matters of sexuality. If she told them the truth, they'd be stunned, but she knew with complete confidence that they wouldn't judge her harshly, would in fact back her up in anything she decided.

She loved them, but that hadn't made it easy fending off their nonsense, all while lost in the reality of the situation.

It felt good to be home.

It felt...something altogether different knowing she'd shortly see her fantasy man again.

He was here, in Buckhorn, where she considered starting over.

He hadn't forgotten her.

*He wanted her to work with him day in and day out.*

Did that mean he hoped to pick up where they'd left off, as if she'd be that easy?

Or did it mean he wasn't interested and spending that much time with her in close proximity wouldn't make him as lust-crazed as it would her?

No, she couldn't believe that. Even Shohn and Adam had noticed his interest. And commented on it. Repeatedly.

"Lisa has an admirer," Shohn had said in a childish singsong voice.

"All the single ladies will be so sad to know he's already hooked," Adam had added while patting a hand over his heart. "Guess I'll just have to console them."

"I think it was love at first sight."

"Wait until he finds out she's smarter than him."

"And more motivated."

"And better paid."

Finally Lisa had willingly gone over the side of the boat, opposite from where they'd cast their fishing lines. Ignoring their calls, she'd swum to shore and pretended to consider walking back until they both begged her not to. If it hadn't been for the cow patties everywhere she tried to step, and the occasional spider web stretched between colorful weeds, she would have walked. But she wasn't an idiot.

Just embarrassed. And overcome with lust. And now even more fixated on her fantasy man.

Gray Neely.

On top of being the sexiest, most gorgeous man she'd ever met, he was also kind and considerate.

He'd willingly let her off the hook, promising not to speak of their previous acquaintance.

He was also macho, a man's man, easily meshing with her brother and cousin. How he'd looked…

She drew in a shuddering breath, filling her lungs with country air, and again pictured him in her mind. Rugged beard stubble. Alert gray eyes, focused on her. Hair longer and more disheveled. Loose board shorts and laceless sneakers, his shirt open, his muscled, hairy chest bare.

Damn, but her mouth watered, and she was so distracted she didn't dock as smoothly as usual. A frog leaped away as she drew a line through the cleat on the dock and secured the boat. A few more deep breaths and, hiking her canvas tote bag over her shoulder, she climbed out of the boat.

From the shadows of the gas pumps three docks down, a deep voice said, "I figured you'd come by water." Shirtless, barefoot, wearing only trunks, he pushed to his feet and strode toward her. His dark hair was wet, slicked back, his sinner's eyelashes spiked, his beard even more noticeable.

He stopped only a few feet from her, his gaze taking a lazy stroll from her braided hair down her body to the flip-flops on her feet. "Whenever I thought of you—and I did, often—I saw you in a business suit, your hair contained, your look professional. I liked that look a lot, especially since it was so different from the woman you became in my room."

A wild woman, that's what he meant, because that's what she'd been. Her breath stalled. "Voices carry," she whispered. "We can't talk here on the lake."

He held out a hand and, feeling as risqué as she had that night a month ago, she took it. God, she remembered his hands, so big and strong, a little rough from work, but warm and gentle as they'd touched her. Everywhere.

Silently he led her up to the store, and with each step she took, her heart jumped harder, faster. Low in her stomach, butterflies battled.

She was thirty years old, but she'd never, not once, experienced desire like this. Only with him.

One of the double doors stood open and as they stepped inside, Gray closed and locked it. Her breath caught and anticipation sharpened.

No lights were on and without the sun coming through the windows, it remained dark...and intimate.

He slowly backed her up to the wall and cupped one hand to the side of her face. "As I was saying."

Lisa felt his breath, the warmth of his big body, and had no idea what he was talking about.

"I like seeing you in these short shorts, and I like your hair like this. You were sexy before, but now you're earthy, too, and I want another taste."

After saying all that, he waited, giving her time.

Lisa nervously, anxiously licked her bottom lip— and saw his gaze sharpen.

"I remember you with short hair," she whispered. "Clean-shaven, polished." She reached up, smoothing back a lock of wet hair that had fallen over his brow. "Now your hair is shaggy, you're already tanned, and this beard scruff..." She coasted her thumb over his bristly jaw, feeling the tease of that rasp deep inside herself. "Not only are you not in a dress shirt, you're shirtless, and honestly, it's making me a little nuts."

"Nuts is good." He moved closer still but didn't quite touch her. "I was waiting on you, remembering how it had been, thinking of how it could be again, and got myself so worked up that I had to jump in the lake to cool down."

Lisa smiled. Little by little, the same chemistry she'd felt that night in the bar came sneaking over her. "I was stunned to see you here."

He nodded. "Stunned, but pleased." Both hands now cupped her face and he murmured huskily, "I've missed you."

It saddened her to say it, but they both needed a reminder of the truth. "You don't even know me."

"Not true." Gray slowly lowered his head until his nose touched her temple. "I know your scent, the feel of your skin, and how you taste."

His lips lightly grazed her cheek, making her shiver.

Near her ear, he whispered, "I know the sounds you make when you come."

She released a shuddering, broken breath.

"Yeah," he said with satisfaction. "That's how it starts." He trailed his fingertips down her shoulder to her elbow, then under her breast and over her frantically pounding heartbeat. "It ends with sweet, rough, broken moans and you holding me tight until the pleasure is over."

The way he said it, she *felt* it. "Yes."

"I want it all. Again."

As his hand covered her breast, his palm teasing her nipple, she nodded and admitted the truth. "Me, too."

"We have an hour." It wasn't long enough, but it was better than nothing. He needed her. Bad.

Right now.

But she didn't move. In fact, she seemed to be holding her breath.

When he looked down at her, Gray saw her eyes closed, her bottom lip caught in her teeth, her expression sweetly agonized.

He continued to cuddle her breast while raining small, damp kisses down her jaw and her throat to her shoulder. Jesus, she smelled good, like the fresh outdoors and musk and every fucking fantasy he'd ever had, all rolled into one.

But damn it, she still didn't say anything, and as bad as he wanted her, he wanted her to feel the same.

Time to rein it in. Wasn't easy, but he asked, "You need some time?"

She nodded, then shook her head, then groaned. "I don't know."

Well, that was answer enough. "It's okay. I can wait." It'd kill him. A dozen times over. But if that's what she needed—

"That night..." Her eyes opened, full of pleading confusion. "That wasn't me."

"It wasn't me, either." He dropped both hands to her waist—safer territory—and put his forehead to hers. "It was just...right. The right time, the right person." He had to kiss her, just once, so he did. Not too deep, but far from a peck. And far from satisfying. "The right thing to do—for both of us."

"I've never done anything like it before."

For a novice, she'd been damn good. Great. Mind-blowing, in fact. "I don't exactly make a habit of it, either." He smiled, realizing something. "I like your name."

Her laugh was muffled against his throat. "I like yours, too."

"I meant what I said." With two fingers under her chin, he brought her face up. "It's nobody's business but ours."

She nodded. "This is my home, Gray. My entire family is here."

"I know. Everywhere I go, I trip over one of them." He kissed her again, all the while telling himself he had to stop that. Except that she kissed him back and damn, that nearly killed his resolve not to push her. He eased back, a little more breathless. Harder. "I like them."

Dazed, her gaze on his mouth, she asked, "Who?"

So cute. So fucking hot. Eventually she'd be his again. He had to believe that. "Your family."

"Oh. Right. Yeah, they're all terrific." Rubbing at her forehead, she admitted, "None of them would ever expect this of me. I've been so singularly focused on my career, I never made much time for relationships."

He paused—and she shot her gaze to his.

"Not that this is a relationship. God, no. I mean..."

He loved how she blushed.

A little desperately, she said, "It was just sex."

"That felt like more?"

Time stretched out with neither of them confirming or denying that.

Until finally, an eternity later, she nodded. "Yes. It felt like more."

Her hand opened on his chest, the touch now familiar, bringing all those other touches to the forefront of his mind. She'd been bold, curious, and she'd burned him up.

He covered her hand with his own. "To me, too." So many times he'd regretted not getting her name or contact info. At the time, both of them had enjoyed the anonymity and the relief of distraction.

He'd realized too late that he wanted more, because she'd already gone. Now that he knew her better and understood what an anomaly it was for her to indulge in a one-night stand, he understood why she hadn't stuck around.

"Will it freak you out to know I thought about you a lot?" Her thick lashes swept down, hiding her eyes, and her voice was barely a whisper. "Every night, but sometimes during the day, too."

He wasn't freaked out at all. Just the opposite. "Glad

to know I wasn't alone in that." Another kiss, this one longer, deeper. *Hot.* He licked his tongue along her bottom lip, then just inside. Her lips parted more, and he sank in, hungry, needing this. Needing her.

She moaned.

"It's okay," he told her as he readjusted, aligning his body to hers, drawing her closer. "It's just a kiss."

"Just a kiss." Her arms came around his neck and, helping with the embrace, she went on tiptoe.

Time slipped away. If he wanted her to work with him—and hell, yeah, he did—he needed to iron out a few details before customers started showing up.

Again cupping her face, he ended the kiss by small degrees, then drew her head to his chest. He gave himself a few seconds to catch his breath and clear the fog of lust before he said, "If I could make another suggestion?"

"Another?"

He liked her braid. It was a little loose, a little sloppy. He ran his hand along the length and enjoyed the silkiness of her hair. "The first being that you work with me."

"Oh, yeah. That."

"Yes, that." He took a step back to see her but kept a hand flattened to the wall beside her head. "And if you agree, then how about we start over?"

She shook her head. "With what?"

"Yesterday is the first day we formally met." And now he had an opportunity to know her, really know her.

Along with her million family members.

Fighting off a laugh ripe with embarrassment, Lisa

covered her mouth and whispered, "We did that without even knowing each other's names."

Liking her laugh—liking *her*—he said, "I know."

She snickered. "'Course you do. You were there."

"There, and very actively participating." Backing up so that he wouldn't pressure her again, Gray leaned a hip on the ice cream case and smiled at her. "I didn't need your name. But everything else..." His smile faded. "I needed the rest of it in a bad way. So thank you. You don't know it, but you turned me around."

Inching closer, she asked, "What does that mean?"

Hard to explain, especially since he didn't entirely understand it, but he gave it a shot. "I was..." He wouldn't say lost. That sounded real pansy-ass. "...at loose ends." *And struggling to get my head on straight.* But again, that made him sound far too weak. "I needed a change, but I'd been resisting and fucking brooding about it and if you hadn't showed up I probably would have gotten shitfaced and then gotten up the next day and carried on as usual. But after you..."

Those big, dark eyes watched him with gentle curiosity. "After me?"

"Everything felt different. Me, my situation."

"What situation is that?"

He shook his head. No way would he lay the heavy stuff on her. Not now, maybe not ever. "I was ready for a change of pace, and so here I am. But I had no idea I'd find you here, too."

She tipped her head and that silky braid fell over her shoulder, the tip resting against her breast. "Shohn and Adam said you were a cop?"

"Yeah." He'd thought to retire from the force when

he hit his midsixties. Not with an injury. Not with rage consuming him. Not with his best friend gone forever.

Now very near, Lisa asked, "Not anymore?"

He shook his head again, but that didn't suffice, so he said, "No."

Her eyes went softer, darker. She touched his arm. "You're from Chicago?"

"No, but my partner was." He pushed off the case, moving away from her and the comfort he didn't deserve, giving her his back. "I'm originally from Cincinnati. I was only in Chicago for his funeral."

He didn't hear Lisa move, but he felt the light touch of her small hand on his back. "I'm sorry."

Done with that subject, Gray turned to face her and gestured at the shop. "The hours are flexible. Minimum wage to start, but I'm open to promoting you if things work out."

Her lips twitched. "Wow, such a…great offer."

"You'll be working with me most of the time."

"There is that."

She considered it a perk? Because he sure as hell did.

As if thinking it out, she began to pace. "Like you said, my family is everywhere, and never, not in a million years, would they ever think I'd do…what we did."

"That just means I know you better than most." He'd already told her it was their secret; she'd either trust him on that or not.

"In some ways, you do. But for the most part, we're still strangers."

Didn't feel that way to him. "We could do a trial run. Take a week or two just to get to know each other." He didn't need that, but it looked as though she did. Patience, he reminded himself.

Her expression perked up. "A trial run? For the job?"

"For us," he explained. "I'd be completely hands-off. That is, unless you say otherwise." Dead serious, he admitted, "The second you say you're ready, I'm full go. But until then, for all anyone will ever know, we just met."

"You'd be doing all the giving."

Heat rolled through him, making his voice gruff. "Believe me, I remember the payoff, and lady, you're well worth the wait."

Again her face warmed, but she smiled. "Gorgeous, generous and a charmer, too. How am I supposed to resist that?"

"You're not. So tell me, Lisa Sommerville. You wanna work for me?"

"You know, Gray Neely, I believe I do."

"Great." Hearing voices outside, he strode to the doors and opened them. "You can start right now."

THE MORNING WENT off without a hitch. It was, in fact, enjoyable to jump in on one of the busiest days on the lake. As a kid, Lisa had been to the shop so many times that she knew the layout, which hadn't changed much, caught on quick to restocking and enjoyed her turn at refueling the boats.

It also impressed her how Gray handled things. He was friendly with the customers, making an effort to remember names and relationships, deferential with the elders, patient with the kids and judicious with the flirting hordes of women who descended on him.

Okay, so maybe there weren't actual hordes. But

there *were* a lot of them, and to her dismay, none of them appeared to need time to think about it. Most of the women were unknown to her, vacationers there for the summer or maybe just a day.

But a few others were women she'd grown up with. Even April and Kady, two of her uncle Gabe's beautiful blond bombshell daughters, came in.

It was a joke in the family, how her uncle Gabe had been such a handful and a ladies' man and now all three of his daughters were miniature, more feminine versions of him, which meant they turned heads everywhere they went.

Gray, however, treated them with the same reserved, respectful politeness he used with the rest of the women.

All except her. With her, he smiled more warmly, and more often. And she caught him constantly watching her. Each and every time their gazes met, she felt the heat and need like a growing, combustible force.

Did she dare indulge in another fling with him?

Did she have the willpower to resist?

Later that day, around suppertime, her uncle Morgan's daughter, Amber, showed up. The opposite of Kady and April, Amber had long, sleek dark hair and amazing blue eyes. Also unlike Kady and April, Amber wore a sundress instead of a bikini. She still looked like a model, and Lisa still felt drab in comparison.

Amber spoke to Gray only for a minute, then swooped in on Lisa. "You're really working here?"

On tiptoe, straightening the shelf of hats that had been displaced by customers, Lisa nodded. "I really am."

"For the whole summer?"

Knowing Amber and recognizing that tone, Lisa turned to face her cousin. "That's the plan, but Amber, seriously, do *not* start playing matchmaker."

At that, Gray looked up and, frowning, put aside some receipts and headed toward them.

"But I have the perfect guy! Actually about a dozen perfect guys."

"No."

"Don't be a stick in the mud. You always work and never have time, but if you're right here anyway, you at least have to meet them." Holding up a hand, Amber insisted, "I won't take no for an answer. A casual meet and greet, that's all. I know! I'll invite them over to the Sunday family picnic."

Nearly every Sunday her entire family gathered together. Both her uncle Sawyer and her uncle Morgan had houses near the lake. Her cousin Casey did, too, but his was smaller, not really equipped for the big crowds of her far-reaching clan.

Dreading the possibility of having some hapless guy pushed on her, Lisa turned to Gray and said, "Sorry, but I already promised Gray that I'd work on Sunday."

Amber's face fell.

Gray slid right in there. "It's true. I'm sorry. I didn't realize there was a special function." When Amber gave him a speculative look, he shrugged. "Sundays are busy for us."

"Hmm." Amber didn't look convinced. "We all get together on Sundays. That is, anyone who isn't busy. Uncle Sawyer sometimes has patients, and Dad sometimes has business out of town that won't wait. But around Buckhorn, most everyone closes down on Sundays."

"Not the vacationers."

"No, they're always around, and they never think to get what they need before Sunday." Amber looked from Gray to Lisa and back again. "How many days a week will Lisa work?"

Lisa said quickly, "I like to stay busy. You know that."

"Mmm-hmm. So…five days?" Amber's blue eyes measured them both. "Every day?"

Lisa had no idea where Amber was going with this, only that she was definitely going somewhere. How to answer? Very unsure, she said, "Um…yes?"

"Every day. Wow. You really are a workhorse." Turning to Gray, she added silkily, "Lucky you."

Gray frowned. "When she needs time off, I'll do my best to accommodate her."

"But not this Sunday," Lisa rushed to clarify.

"No worries." Looking smug, Amber gave her a hug, turned to pat Gray on the shoulder and on her way out, said, "I'll see you around."

As soon as her cousin cleared the doorway, Lisa dropped back against the shelves with a groan.

"Trouble?" Gray asked.

"If you knew Amber, you wouldn't have to ask."

"Don't worry about it." Gray, innocent and unaware, said, "What can she possibly do?"

## *CHAPTER THREE*

EVERY. SINGLE. DAY. For a week. An entire week!

That's how long Gray had to suffer through seeing each eligible guy in Buckhorn County paraded through his store for Lisa's approval.

Amber changed it up to keep them guessing, one day coming first thing, then during lunch, once toward suppertime, and so on. Lisa couldn't plan ahead to avoid her, because she never knew when Amber might show up with the hopeful swain in tow.

Each time Lisa was unfailingly polite to the guy without offering encouragement, while also giving her cousin death stares. The guys weren't deterred. Not that Gray blamed them.

Lisa was a catch. Although the better he got to know her, the more he realized that she didn't know it.

The week that Gray had hoped to use to win her over had instead been consumed with Amber's antics.

On the Monday of the following week, Gray waited for Lisa outside, determined to catch her before she reached the front door and dug into her duties. It was easy to see how she'd advanced in the business world. She wasn't afraid of hard work, seemed tireless and got things done with little fuss and efficient grace.

He liked it that each day she came to work by boat, even once when it rained. Yes, she was a polished, sophisticated and accomplished businesswoman. But she was also nature's child, earthy and real, not afraid of getting soaked by a summer storm.

When necessary, she waded thigh-deep into lake weeds, getting mud between her toes. She helped a kid unhook a fish, showed another how to bait his hook, explained the proper attachment of a ski line to a family of five and launched a boat for a vacationer who'd never done it before. Gray had stared in mixed awe and pride as she'd backed the car and trailer down the ramp, put the car in Park and then gone around and released the brand-new boat, using a lead line to position it alongside the dock, then tied it off.

While the owner of the boat, his wife and three kids stood there watching, Lisa pulled the car out and parked it in the lot, returned the man's keys and waved off his gratitude.

Astounding. And sexy. A take-charge woman got him every time.

Granted, he'd rather she put all that energy and focus to work in the bedroom, or on the kitchen table—hell, the dock at night, with the stars overhead, would suit him just fine.

The better he knew her, the more he liked her. The more he liked her, the more he wanted her.

In so many ways, she surprised him. Good surprises.

In a short time he'd learned that Lisa wasn't afraid of fish, worms, snakes, turtles or any of the things he was used to women screeching over. However, she kept a respectful distance from spiders. The one time she'd requested he deal with an insect, she hadn't wanted it killed, just relocated outside.

He loved how she laughed, how she analyzed a shelf before filling it to best utilize the space and how she dusted her hands off on her very perfect rear end.

He even liked how she looked when perturbed, as she sometimes was when she felt people weren't making safe choices.

This week, he decided, would be different. He'd manage more than small talk. At the very least, he'd steal another kiss. Or two. And if that worked out, well, who knew?

So that Monday morning, Gray waited on the end of the dock, his bare feet dangling in the tepid water. Anticipation thrummed through his bloodstream as he listened to the familiar purr of a motor drawing near.

Lisa was early.

Standing, he stared ahead, sexual tension ramping up, and then he saw the small boat cutting through the glassy surface of the lake. It caused a rippling wake that stirred the reflection of the bright lemon sunrise behind her. Her honey-blond hair glowed with the light of dawn and she looked so sweet, so damned serene.

Damn, he needed to have her again. Soon.

She lifted a hand when she saw him, her lush mouth curling into a smile. While a giant heron soared overhead and carp lazily crested the water, she parked the boat and tossed him a line. He secured the front and she tied off the back.

Small docks lined the entire shoreline of the marina's property to accommodate boaters coming in for supplies or gas, or for those who hung out to fish. Lisa had made a habit of parking at the one farthest away. That left them beneath several towering elms that offered shade to midday fishermen.

He extended a hand and Lisa took it, allowing him to help her out of the boat and onto the dock.

Today, with her usual shorts and flip-flop sandals, she wore a peach-colored camisole top that laced up the front and sported a loosely tied bow at the top. The outfit was innocently provocative and made him burn.

Keeping her hand in his, he looked her over with appreciation. "You left your hair loose."

With her free hand, she touched it, smoothing one side behind her ear. "I envy Amber and Gabe's daughters. They all have such gorgeous hair."

Hotter by the second, he said, "As do you."

A crooked smile showed her uncertainty. "There's no comparison and you know it. Amber's hair is dark enough that it has blue highlights in the sun. Kady, April and Brianna are the opposite, blondes so pale it's hard to believe the color is real. But me, I'm just... wishy-washy dark blonde. And no, I'm not fishing for a compliment, just stating the obvious."

"Then I'll state the obvious, too." He brushed his thumb over her knuckles. "There's not a single thing wishy-washy about you. I love your hair. How it looks and how it feels." He kept remembering the feel of it in his hands as he rode her slow and deep, and each time he got semihard. But he kept that part to himself. "Your hair inspires fantasies."

Her laugh told him she didn't believe him. "Thank you. It's not that I'm insecure."

About most things, he'd agree. But there was something, some hidden uncertainty, when she talked about her family. "No?"

She shook her head. "It's just that the clan is made

up of some really great genes. But that wouldn't affect me."

Not understanding, Gray decided it'd be best discussed with more privacy. "Come here." He led her to a bench halfway up the hill, away from the water that echoed every word. Tugging her down beside him, he asked, "Okay, why wouldn't it affect you?"

"My family?" She smiled again. "You fit in so perfectly, I forget you're not from around here and don't know. See, Dad married Mom when I was six. I'm family, 100 percent, but I'm not blood related."

He recalled Shohn mentioning it, that her mother had married when she was still young, so she'd grown up in the area. "So Jordan is your stepfather?"

"Technically. But Adam and I don't think of him that way. He's just... Dad."

"I'm glad." Unable to stop himself, Gray stared at her mouth. "So he's happy to have you home?"

"Everyone is." She wrinkled her nose. "I'm the oddity, you know. Once, ages ago, my cousin Casey lived away from Buckhorn for a while. But it didn't last. The rest have always been more than content to settle here. They're all supportive, but they've never understood why I ventured away."

"Do you know why?"

Troubled, she shrugged, looked away. "Not really."

Gray teased a kiss over her temple and that brought her attention back to him. He smiled. "You liked your job?"

"I loved my job." She sighed. "Right up until I didn't."

"What changed?"

"I don't really know. Instead of feeling pumped

about some of the challenges, I got fatigued. Things would happen and instead of being motivated, I'd get annoyed." She shook her head. "I started getting sick, too."

"Sick how?"

"Bad headaches, nausea." She flattened her mouth. "High blood pressure, too."

Shit.

"And I could never seem to sleep. How dumb is that? Me, the one who thrived on pressure, getting stressed out." Making a face, she whispered, "It made me feel weak."

"Only because you're so strong."

She laughed. "I didn't feel strong. I felt pathetic. Like a stranger in my own skin. Does that make sense?"

"Yeah, it does." Because that's how he'd felt, too—until he met her. He lifted her hand, kissed her palm. "You're okay now?"

"Yes." She drew a bolstering breath. "Ever since that night with you, the night I decided I needed a big change, I've been more relaxed, sleeping better. Well, mostly sleeping better. But sometimes…"

"Sometimes what?"

"Sometimes *you*."

Gray studied her, how the morning sunlight shone on her face. "You said you still think about that night."

"Think about it, dream about it. About you." She stared at him with those dark, consuming eyes, then sighed. "A lot."

"It was memorable for me as well."

Suddenly antsy, she pushed to her feet and walked to a tree, leaning on the trunk while watching him.

"We were supposed to use this time to get to know each other."

Gray stood but didn't approach her. "I did."

"How? We've been swamped."

"You think I haven't paid attention? Not for a second am I ever unaware of you."

Her gaze locked on his. "I've seen you watching me."

"I can't help myself." He didn't point out the obvious, that she knew because she'd been watching him, too. "I know you like two cups of coffee first thing in the morning."

Her mouth slipped into a smile. "True." Her gaze flickered to his chest, then away. "I know that you only shave every third day."

"Unless there's a special occasion." Nice that she'd noticed. And given her interest in his chest, he wished he hadn't pulled on a T-shirt. "It bothers you?"

"I think it's sexy."

"Now, see? I know that you're honest, too. That you say what's on your mind."

"Actually, I didn't mean to." Again her gaze dipped to his body and she let out a breath. "Around you, I just forget myself."

He smiled. "I figured out, pretty quickly, that you know a hell of a lot more about boats than I do."

Playing along, she said, "I figured out that you're a quick learner." She didn't leave it there. Brows together, she added, "And you have a knack for just *knowing* things. Like, you look at a trolling motor and somehow figure out that the propeller got tangled in lake weeds. Or that the breaker had blown on the freezer chest—and how to fix it. Or the most expedient way to get a fishing line out of a tree."

"Those were all common sense."

"A rare commodity."

"And you?" Slowly, not wanting to push her, Gray moved closer. "Is there anything you can't do?"

Her chin lifted. "I can read instructions, so no. Unless it involves brute strength." She flexed her arm, showing a small biceps. "It's the truth, I lack muscle."

Sliding his fingers around her slender arm, he tugged her closer. "I have a feeling that, if necessary, you'd figure that out, too."

Staring up at him, she whispered, "There's usually a way."

"Would it be rushing things too much if I kissed you?"

She breathed a little faster. "I was hoping you would." And before Gray could make a move, she came against him, her arms around his neck pulling him down, her mouth lifting to his.

Sweet. *And hot.* He tangled a hand in her loose hair, keeping her close, turning his head for a better fit.

She made a soft sound and opened her mouth. He felt her tongue and gave her his own.

Scooping his other arm around her waist, he arched her into him. It wasn't enough, not when he wanted, needed, to be inside her again, hearing her fast breaths and small cries, feeling the clench of her body as she neared release…

Tires on gravel alerted them both and they jumped apart.

Lisa looked startled, her hair mussed, her lips swollen.

He blew out a breath. Damn it, he had a boner. "Stay

put and I'll deal with it." Pulling his shirt out and down to cover himself, he headed for the building.

Her cousin Amber exited her truck with yet another man.

Jesus, where did she find all the guys? Did she recruit them from out of the county?

Pasting on a smile, he said, "Amber. Hi."

"Hey, Gray." She slid a look over him and gave a very knowing smile. "Dave and I were headed into town and I figured I'd stop to say hi to Lisa. Is she here yet?"

"I'm not sure," he lied, and eyed the guy.

"Dave and Lisa went to school together."

"Is that right?" Like he gave a shit? Why did Amber persist in throwing men at her cousin? If the men were that great, she should keep them for herself. "You live around here, Dave?"

"Next county over."

Well, hell. Amber was bringing them in!

"I'm here visiting my mom. I didn't know Lisa was back. And working here?" He laughed. "Hard to believe."

It occurred to Gray that Amber still watched him. Waiting for his reaction to that possible insult? Gray smiled again. "Pretty sure she could work anywhere she wants, but yeah, she's helping out."

Dave rubbed his hands together. "When do you expect her?"

Lisa came around the corner. She'd smoothed her hair and straightened that sexy top, but her lips still looked thoroughly kissed and damn, he wanted her.

Dave probably did, too, the dick.

"Hey, Dave," Lisa said. Just that, nothing more.

"Lisa!" He took a step forward, his gaze gobbling her up. "It's so great to see you. How've you been?"

"Busy." She kept walking, right past Dave and right up to her cousin, where she hooked her arm and began dragging her away. "If you guys will excuse us a moment?"

Amber looked back at Gray and laughed. In triumph? Sounded like.

Hands in his pockets, Gray eyed Dave. "So."

Dave kept staring after the women. "She looks good."

"Yeah."

"Last time I saw her, she was all buttoned up in a business suit."

*Bet she looked sexy as hell, too.* "When was that?"

"Few years ago. We were both out of town and ran into each other."

"Got to catch up?"

"Not really. She had a grueling schedule to keep."

*Good.*

The women returned. Lisa, utterly serene, said, "Dave, it was nice seeing you."

Confused by that dismissal, Dave said, "Uh..."

"I need to get to work now."

Amber kept grinning. "Come on, Dave. We don't want to hold them up." But as she opened her truck door she said to Gray, "So Sunday. Any chance you can get away?"

Lisa, whipping back around, lost her serenity. "Amber!"

Gray said, "Probably," and hoped like hell he didn't regret it. "I have a part-time guy who helps out when necessary."

Lisa blinked at him. "I didn't know that."

"He's been on a vacation to visit his brother in Texas, but he's due back Wednesday."

"Who?" Lisa demanded, which sort of tickled Gray. For a hotshot businesswoman, she'd really taken a territorial liking to her job at the marina.

"Petie Burkman." And from what Gray could tell, Petie was another veteran of the county. Everyone seemed to know him.

Sure enough, Lisa nodded. "He used to run the garage in town. He has to be in his seventies now."

"Almost his eighties, I think." Petie had the thickest white hair Gray had ever seen, a lot of wrinkles from overexposure to the sun and a lazy way of getting things done. But he was also trustworthy, sharp as a tack and reliable. "He came with the shop when I purchased it."

Lisa took that in, said, "Okay," as if it had needed her approval and then rounded on her cousin again. *"Amber."*

Amber ignored her. "Two o'clock, okay, Gray? Join my family and me and I'll introduce you around, let everyone get to know you better. Lisa can show you where. I'll tell everyone to expect you."

Gray gave it very quick thought, saw Dave staring at Lisa's legs and said, "Sounds good, thanks. Can I bring anything?"

"Your swimming trunks and a smile." Amber practically stuffed Dave into the truck, then got behind the wheel and drove away.

Her dust hadn't yet settled before Lisa groaned. "I'm sorry."

"For?"

"Getting you shanghaied. I told her no more on the man parade and she apparently refocused on you. I should have expected it. Especially after…" Her voice trailed off and she touched her cheek.

Intrigued, Gray asked, "After?"

Lisa sighed and dropped her hand. "After she saw the whisker burn on my cheek."

He tipped her face up, saw the small pink mark and bent to kiss it gently. "She asked?"

"She's Amber. Of course she asked."

"What did you tell her?"

"I think I stared, stammered and then told her to take Dave away and cease with the matchmaking."

"Avoidance and deflection. Guess it didn't work?"

She huffed. "With Amber? Not ever."

"She means well." At least, that was the impression Gray got. Assuming the moment had passed and she was done making out with him, Gray went to the shop door and held it open for Lisa.

"Everyone encourages her, that's the problem." Grumbling, Lisa strode in past him. "Someone should meddle in her love life, let her see how it feels."

Love life? "My family is small, especially compared to yours." Gray figured every family might be small compared to hers. "So clue me in. You and Amber get along or not?"

"Of course! I love her—pushy faults and all." Heading to the coffeepot, she added, "And usually she's dead-on. I mean, Amber is the one who fixed up Shohn with Nadine, and she had a lot to do with Garrett and Zoey getting together."

After chugging down half the coffee, Lisa continued. "Rumor has it Amber even had a hand in Casey's romance with Emma, even though she was only a kid at the time."

"Sounds like she's good at what she does."

Lisa ignored his input. "But she's never been able to accept that I—"

This time her voice dropped like a stone in the lake. "That you what? Were too busy working to get interested?"

Deflated, she stared at the remaining coffee in her cup. "That I've never met anyone interesting enough to get interested."

So he was interesting enough? Because, damn, it sure felt like she was interested.

"Mmm," Lisa said around another drink of coffee. "How is it you do everything so well? Even your coffee is excellent."

"Lisa?"

She peeked at him and said, "What?"

"That kiss."

Her expression softened, her eyes going darker, sultry—just as he remembered. "You did that really, *really* well."

Behind them a family walked in, chatting. When Gray glanced that way he saw the mom, the dad and even the kid were decked out in clichéd fishing gear, which meant they were novices, because all the seasoned fishermen knew better than to wear hats full of hooks.

With free time gone, he turned back to Lisa.

Those soul-sucking eyes of hers were steady on his face. "We were supposed to be getting to know each other better."

Gray nodded.

"But you're right. I know you." She closed the space between them, put a hand to his chest, and whispered, "I wish we'd had more time."

Well, damn. How was he supposed to work after she said that?

"You owe me a second cup." And with that she up-ended her coffee to finish it off, patted his chest and started for the family. Watching her sassy walk, it took a second before Gray grinned. He'd made headway.

So now all he needed was more time.

## *CHAPTER FOUR*

HAD HE REALLY left the force for a slower pace? Didn't feel like it. The first three days of the second week with Lisa had been nothing short of insane. Vacationers flocked to the lake, and more than half of them had no clue about boating safety and lake regulations.

A bunch of college kids had shown up with a pontoon that they planned to drastically overload. The cop in him came out and he'd refused to let them launch—which had caused a scene with thirteen pissed-off college idiots who were already lit at ten in the morning.

Gray hadn't seen Lisa disappear, but a few minutes later her uncle Morgan, the freaking mayor, was there with the sheriff, and Gray had taken satisfaction in being able to back off and let others handle it.

Lisa did introductions immediately afterward. Gray liked the sheriff. Tucker Turley gave off a mild-mannered, won't-get-riled vibe that he quietly backed up with pure steel. It was actually entertaining to watch.

He also learned that her uncle, who had once been sheriff before being elected mayor, now headed up the COCP program, or Community Organized Crime Prevention. Made up of local agencies, which included Shohn as a ranger and Garrett as a firefighter, as well as area residents, the COCP coordinated to fight minor crime, delinquency, vandalism and such.

Nice that her uncle cared enough to stay so involved, and because of that he wielded a lot of respect and confidence.

Turley, much younger, had the badge but didn't seem to mind Morgan's input—which proved Turley was confident and smart. Better to work with Morgan than fight against him.

Being the authority figure, Gray knew, was hard to shake. It got in your blood, settled into your bones and stuck.

Just yesterday, early evening, some yahoo had decided to teach a ten-year-old kid how to swim by throwing him in without a jacket. He'd heard Lisa yell, a bigger splash, and seconds later she'd waded out with her arm protectively around the shaken kid, who was still coughing up lake water. Already headed toward them, Gray watched her gently seat the boy on a bench, then whirl in a fury on the man. She'd poked his chest, crowded into his space and snapped loud enough for everyone on the lake to hear, *"Are you an idiot?"*

With a lot of audacity, the guy had yelled back, "Mind your own damn business, lady!"

Gray hadn't remembered moving, but in a heartbeat he was between them, so pissed that breathing wasn't easy. Through his teeth, he'd growled, "Back it down. Now."

The guy had, but before Gray could say anything more a woman appeared. She was even more pissed than Gray. From what he could figure, the man was a disappointing blind date and the lady was already done with him. After chewing the guy up one side and down the other, she'd put a life preserver on her son, gotten him in the boat—which was apparently hers, not his—and she took off...leaving the man still on shore.

Smug, Lisa had watched him head for his car. When he'd realized he didn't have the keys, he launched into another fit. He'd even kicked the car.

Scowling, Lisa had headed for him, but Gray cut her off. "No." She tried to go around him, so he'd stopped her again. "I'll deal with it."

Gray had watched the hesitation in her eyes, then saw the trust. "Okay."

The confrontation hadn't gone well. The guy had blustered and shouted and caused a scene. Gray kept his cool.

Finally, with some vague threats, the man stomped off. Where he'd gone, Gray didn't know, but as long as he left, it didn't matter to him.

Lisa had smiled at him, patted his chest, and just that easily she'd gone back to helping other folks. When the woman and her son returned near dark, she'd taken the time to thank both Lisa and Gray. Blind dates, she declared, were off her agenda forever. She'd hugged her son, a cute little boy, and said she'd be back again. Gray and Lisa both waved her off, and they hadn't had a chance to talk about it since.

Luckily, the mishaps after that were simple ones, easily corrected. But he made a note to stock up on life preservers and to post a large sign sharing navigation rules and a required equipment chart.

Now here it was, the butt crack of dawn on the fourth day, and Gray, wearing running shorts and sneakers with a loose T-shirt and a backward ball cap, headed up the walk to Lisa's house. That she had a house didn't surprise him; she was a very resourceful, intelligent and capable woman.

But from what he understood, she hadn't stayed in Buckhorn much. Maybe the house meant that, deep down, she'd always intended to settle back home at some point.

He hoped so.

He'd gotten her address from Amber, who still stopped by the marina at least every other day but, thankfully, no longer dragged other dudes along. His plan was simple—spend more alone time with Lisa without pressuring her. From what Amber had said, Lisa got enough pressure from everyone else. Her massive family wanted her to put down roots, and they weren't shy in attempting to sway her.

For once the skies were cloudy and the air smelled of rain. He knew fishing boats would flock to the lake, but there'd be fewer skiers, and for today, at least, he liked that trade-off.

If he caught Lisa before her jog, he could join her. It wasn't an intimate dinner, and it was a far cry from sex, but at least they wouldn't have half the lake's population crowded around them.

Assuming what her brother and cousin had said was true, she jogged each morning. To do that, she'd have to already be up and about. And if she wasn't yet up and he woke her...maybe that'd be okay, too. Gray pictured her all drowsy and sleep rumpled and had to fight off a boner.

When he had his hand raised to knock on her front door, it suddenly opened and Lisa rushed out, almost plowing into him.

He caught her upper arms, then winced from her short, startled scream. "Hey, it's just me."

Wide-eyed, she blinked him into focus, then shoved him back and put a hand to her heart. "Gray! What in the world are you doing here? You scared me half to death."

He took in her fitted running clothes and felt the slow burn of desire. "I was hoping to jog with you."

The hand went from her heart to her high, sloppy ponytail. "But... I don't like anyone to see me like this. It's why I jog so early."

"It's just me."

Expression droll, she said, "You're at the top of the list of people who should never see me wrecked."

"You're not wrecked." Far from it. "The shorts are hot."

Her laugh teased over him as she looked down at her pink gym shorts. "Hot, huh?"

"Mostly because of the ass inside them. And the legs." He slid a hand to her waist. "And I could totally envy that sports bra."

"Envy?"

"It's holding your rack all snug."

Grinning, she stepped past him and pulled her door shut. "You realize that now you really do have to jog."

"You think I can't?" Did she consider him a slacker?

"With your bod?" She snorted. "I'm sure you aren't afraid of exercise."

"Actually, I like it." Before his leg injury he used to jog regularly. Anticipating the run, he looked around the dark neighborhood. "Where do you jog, anyway?"

"I start here, go up through the school yard, circle

around to the main street, then back. It only takes forty minutes or so."

"Thought you didn't want to be seen."

With a chuckle, she elbowed him. "This is Buckhorn, Gray, not the city. Other than the grocery, which now stays open overnight, the businesses don't open until ten, later on Saturday, and not at all on Sunday. The farmers will be up and about, but we won't see them. Uncle Morgan might be at the courthouse, and Uncle Gabe sometimes starts early if he has a lot to get done. Dad's vet clinic is farther out and Uncle Sawyer still works from home."

"Question—unless I misunderstood, your uncles are brothers, so why do they all have different last names?"

"Caught that, did you? Well, it's easy enough. Uncle Sawyer and Uncle Morgan are the oldest, and they're both Hudsons. Their dad died when they were really young and my grandma remarried and had my dad. But apparently things didn't work out and they divorced. He took off and Dad's never really known him. Then my grandma remarried again and had Uncle Gabe, and she and Grandpa Brett are still together."

"I haven't met her."

"They live in Florida but make it up here several times a year. Stick around and I'm sure you'll have the pleasure." Smiling fondly, Lisa headed for the sidewalk. "Grandma is something. A small, sweet dynamo."

"Sounds like someone else I know."

Brows angled, she asked, "Who?"

He laughed. "You."

"But I told you, we're not blood related."

"There are a lot of things more important than blood."

She thought about that a second, then nodded.

Gray followed her out to the sidewalk, filled his lungs with the clean, storm-thick air and stretched. "I like it here."

Gaze on his body, she said, "Me, too."

But did she like it for the long haul? He hoped so. "Your house is nice." Big enough for a family, but still cozy. Well-trimmed shrubs, flowering annuals and perennials brightened the midsized white ranch with a slate-gray roof and matching shutters. She had a big yard with a few mature trees and a really nice porch holding two rockers.

"Thanks. I bought it as an investment, you know? But since I've been back, I've done some decorating and now it feels more like mine."

"When?" She'd been working with him from sunup to sundown. Whenever he tried to give her a break, she refused.

"When what?"

"When would you have had time to decorate?" Sometimes he suspected she used the marina as a hideout from her imposing and often demonstrative family.

Rather than answer, she started off at an easy lope. Gray held back, enjoying the view. Her ponytail bounced—as did her bottom. Her legs were strong but sleek. Her waist small. Her shoulders straight.

Not once did she look back for him, so he caught up and then metered his pace to match hers. He enjoyed the rhythmic slapping of sneakers on pavement, the way they fell into an easy cadence together. Lisa had a nice, even stride, long for her height.

"In the evenings," she said, not even a little breathless, "I do online shopping. It takes me a while to unwind when I get home, so whenever something new has arrived, curtains or wall art or whatever, I unpack it and put it up."

"I wouldn't mind helping you with that."

She just smiled. "Thanks."

Hell, he'd like to help her with anything, just to spend more time with her. "If you need time off, just tell me."

"I will." They went another block in silence before she spoke again. "I'm very undecided about so many things. It helps to stay busy."

A perfect opening. "I could help with that, too, without you being on the clock."

"Yeah?" She flashed him a grin. "What did you have in mind?"

Only half under his breath, he said, "If I told you everything on my mind, you'd probably slap me."

Eyes straight ahead, she said, "Doubtful, since it's on my mind as well."

"It?"

"Us." She peeked at him, then jogged across the street at a crosswalk in front of the middle school.

Gray caught up to her again. "Think we need to do anything about it?"

"Yes."

He stopped for a heartbeat, but Lisa didn't. Again he quickened his pace to rejoin her. He liked her profile, the very slight smile showing, how her long lashes left shadows on her cheeks. How her breasts jiggled a little despite being squished by the sports bra. "Okay, when?"

She kept going, pushing herself harder, but eventually said, "I like it that you want me. That you know a part of me no one else knows."

No one? Meaning no other guy? "I'm trying to be patient, honey, you know that. Just know that it's not easy, okay?"

"Other women have made offers."

He shrugged. "Other men have made offers."

She shot him a look. "To you?"

Laughing, he shook his head. "To *you*."

"Oh." She waved that off as if it didn't matter.

"Not interested?" he asked. "Not even a little?"

"Not even a little."

That was something, anyway. "Same here." He let that sink in, then added, "I want you. Only you." And for her, he was willing to wait. "Just so you know."

"You don't make it easy."

*All's fair in love and war.* "I'm pushing too much?"

She shook her head. "No, you're just too damned irresistible." Lengthening her stride, she tried to leave him, but he just grinned and kept pace and shortly, a little winded, she slowed again.

They entered the town, lit by stately lampposts lining the street. Weak rays of sunrise couldn't quite penetrate the heavy gray clouds. A light sprinkle started, sending steam to rise from the heated pavement. Lisa didn't mention it, so Gray didn't, either.

They passed an old-fashioned post office, a grocery, an ice cream shop. Lights shone inside the diner, but it wasn't yet open, and sure enough, her uncle Morgan had just pulled into the courthouse. Spotting them, he paused as he got out of his utility vehicle, then started toward them.

"He sees us," Gray told Lisa.

She kept her nose down and kept going.

"He's walking out to greet us."

"Pretend you don't see him," she muttered.

Yeah, right. A man of Morgan Hudson's size and presence would be impossible not to see. "Sorry, can't. It'd make me look both chickenshit and rude."

"Damn it." Slowing her pace, Lisa looked up and smiled brightly, as if only then seeing the big bruiser.

"Faker," Gray whispered.

"Hush." And then, louder, she said, "Uncle Morgan, hi."

Morgan gave his niece a double take and laughed. "The words are right, honey, but the inflection is off. I gather you were hoping to miss me?"

"No, of course not. I always enjoy seeing you."

"'Cept when you have a swain keeping pace?" Morgan slanted his attention to Gray.

Lisa said quickly, "I work for him."

"I know that. Also know Amber tried to fix you up a few times, but you weren't having it."

Lisa groaned.

Gray smiled and offered his hand. "Nice to see you again, Mayor."

Taking his hand, her uncle indulged in an easy greeting without any of the usual fist-crunching, pissing-contest nonsense. "Morgan'll do. 'Specially since Amber tells me you're joining us this Sunday."

"Yes, sir."

"I looked you up." Finally, Morgan freed his hand. "You were a damn good cop. Shame what happened. I see your leg is okay now?"

Aware of Lisa watching him, Gray stiffened. "I'm fine."

"Yeah, that's how I'd tell it, too." Morgan didn't leave. In fact, he scrutinized Gray. "I was especially sorry to read about your partner."

"Thank you."

Lisa half stepped in front of her uncle. "What happened to your leg?"

Gray pulled off his cap, ran a hand through his hair, then replaced it—this time facing forward. "It's nothing."

She rounded on Morgan. "Spill it."

"Not my story to tell, honey." Morgan caught her shoulders, held her still for a loud kiss on the forehead, then stepped back. "I'll let you two finish your jog. But Gray?"

Gray lifted a brow.

"Everyone's looking forward to Sunday. Don't chicken out."

Lisa groaned.

Gray stiffened even more. "Wouldn't miss it."

Laughing, Morgan said, "Yeah, I think you'll do."

Gray watched the mayor stride away because that was easier than meeting Lisa's curious gaze. "Ready to finish this jog?"

"Gray?" She touched his arm.

"You need a break?"

Sighing, she trailed her hand up his arm to his biceps, where she lingered a moment, then to his shoulder. Right there on the sidewalk in front of the courthouse with her uncle not that far away, she stroked over his chest. "This is one of those times where we could get better acquainted."

"Shit." He scrubbed a hand over his face. He didn't like talking about himself, not when talking about Lisa would be far more interesting. But she stood there with those mesmerizing dark eyes and he caved. "You didn't notice the scar on my thigh the night we got together?"

"You were naked," she said as if that explained it. "I was taking in the whole package."

He lifted a brow.

Face flushed, she said, "Not *that* package. I mean…" More color filled her cheeks. "I liked that, too."

Grinning, Gray folded his arms and gave her his undivided attention.

She huffed out a breath. "I liked all of it. Of *you*, I mean. Maybe…too much?"

Too much? Not possible.

Throwing up her hands, she said, "You're gorgeous. You know that. And your body…"

When she shivered, he felt it in his dick. "Any time you want a second showing, let me know."

"I think I do."

His heart tried to punch out of his chest. "Yeah?"

"Will you show me your leg?"

"Sure." Given the wound was high, damn near to his groin, he'd have to get naked, which suited him just fine. "My leg. Both legs. Top to bottom, yours to view. Or touch. Whatever you have in mind…"

Laughing, she swatted him but quickly sobered. "Come on."

He fell into a jog beside her.

"Will you at least tell me how it happened?"

He didn't want to. Hell, he hated talking about it. But given he wanted to know everything about her, it only seemed fair. "Yeah."

"When?"

"When I'm showing you my leg."

She laughed again. "Okay, then. How about tonight?"

He stopped. So did she.

Searching her face, he said, "Tonight works."

Her voice lowered, went as husky as his. "Okay."

Damn, she kept him wired. And confused. "Are we talking about *talking*, or—"

"Well, this looks serious."

They both jumped, turned as one, and found another of her relatives grinning at them through an open truck window.

Gray bit back his groan.

Lisa slapped on another false smile. "Uncle Gabe."

Gabe laughed. "Know what, Lisa? You sound just like I used to when Mom busted me." He eyed them both. "Planning some hanky-panky?"

"Uncle Gabe!"

"Hey, I'm told Gray is staying in Buckhorn, so if he's the lure that keeps you here, it's okay by me. Long as he's a nice guy." Expression changing, Gabe zeroed in on him. "You a nice guy, Gray?"

He didn't miss the warning in the question. "When being nice is appropriate, sure."

Gabe held his gaze for a few beats, then laughed. "I like him, honey. Carry on." Stepping on the gas, Gabe drove away.

"Can't walk a block without tripping over a damned relative."

Gray grinned at her. "They're protective."

"And gossipy, too. Gabe and Morgan will tell Dad

and Sawyer and they'll all tell their wives and everyone in the entire family will think we have a thing."

Gray raised his hand. "Guilty." He had a thing all right. More than a thing. He just needed to get Lisa on board. But until she made up her mind about whether or not to stay in Buckhorn, he didn't want to put her on the spot.

Because he was staying.

Before she could ask all those questions he saw in her gaze, Gray said, "Now, about us getting together again." He brushed the backs of his fingers over her cheek. "I can have Petie close up tonight so we can both get off at seven. What do you think?"

"I think everyone in Buckhorn is going to know."

Probably. From what he could tell, word traveled fast. Challenging her, he asked, "How old are you?"

"Thirty."

"I'm thirty-two. That makes us both old enough to do whatever we damn well please."

Her breath shuddered out. "Oh, Gray." Eyes dark and heated and seductive, she whispered, "We pleased an awful lot."

Yeah, and it ate him up thinking about it. "Damn, baby. Don't look at me like that."

"Like what?"

"Like you're remembering everything and wanting a repeat. I can't get hard, not here on the street in running shorts." He cupped her face, tipped it up to his. "Now tell me we have a date regardless of who will know."

The lustful haze lifted with her smile. "It doesn't bother me if it doesn't bother you."

"Doesn't bother me even a little." All that mattered was having her again.

For the longest time she stared up at him, and finally she laughed. "You're a brave man, Gray Neely. Sexy, nice and brave. I hope you know what you're getting into."

## *CHAPTER FIVE*

Around lunchtime, when the shop finally cleared out, Lisa came over with the last few bites of a microwaved taco and a can of cola, and she hopped her sexy behind up onto the counter beside Gray. Which, of course, guaranteed he wouldn't get anything else done.

Today she wore actual cutoffs frayed along the very tops of her thighs and a sleeveless red blouse. His own adorable, hotter-than-hell country bumpkin.

As he pushed aside a few catalogs of summer gear, she asked, "My place or yours?"

He trailed one finger down her arm. "My place is closer."

Looking back at the door to the stairs, she asked, "How close?"

He pointed up to the ceiling.

She rearranged the wrapper on her taco to get the last bite. "Have you really thought this through?"

"Yes." No hesitation. He knew exactly what he wanted: her.

As if he hadn't spoken, she pointed out, "Because my family has noticed you. And that means they'll bring on the pressure and have all these expectations, and while I might not be here, you say you will be."

"Definitely." And he hoped she'd stick around, too.

As she'd said, her family was here. She had a house. Would that be enough?

"So do you really want to deal with that?"

He wanted to deal with her. "I'm a big boy. Don't worry about me."

"But—"

"Lisa." Leaving the chair, he walked around to stand in front of her. He took the empty wrapper from her hand and pitched it toward the garbage can.

She watched it land inside. "Good shot."

Gray set her Coke aside, then flattened his hands on the counter at either side of her hips. "You can't talk me out of what I want, but if it's not what you want, you can tell me. I'll deal with it."

She stared at his mouth. "I want you."

Much as he loved that, he asked, "But?"

"Everything is so complicated."

"Doesn't have to be."

Suddenly she put her arms around him and hugged him tight. "I don't want to leave you with a mess."

He wanted to say, *Then don't leave.* But he was determined not to push her on that. She needed to make her own decision—and he'd help by making Buckhorn more enticing.

Smoothing her hair, he said, "I can handle your family." He hoped.

She laughed and hugged him tighter. "Oh, you poor misguided man."

Okay, so he was being pretty optimistic about that. But he'd routinely handled petty thugs and hard-core criminals, prosecutors and defense attorneys, even stubborn-as-hell judges. How bad could her family be? "Trust me."

The air around them seemed to crackle. She snuggled closer, kissed his throat and said, "I think I always have."

That did it for him.

Giving her time to object, Gray slowly parted her thighs and stepped between them, then, with his hands on her trim hips, he snugged her up close so their bodies meshed.

*"Gray,"* she whispered before melting against him.

"Damn." He kissed her throat, her shoulder, over to her jaw.

Hands tight on his shoulders, she sought his mouth with hers. When their lips touched, they both went still, but not for long. Sinking a hand into her hair, Gray kept her close and nudged her lips open, turned his head for a better angle, sank his tongue in to taste and tease. *This.* He'd needed this a lot. But only with her.

The kiss went hot and wet and deep. But it wasn't enough, not even close. The better he knew her, the more he thought forever wouldn't be enough. She gave a soft groan, arched into him—

A noise sounded behind them.

Taken off guard—something that never happened—Gray jerked around, blocking her with his body. What he saw left him blank.

Not customers. No one from her family.

Just a stray dog.

Relieved that he hadn't let Lisa get caught in a compromising situation that might've embarrassed her, Gray took in the ancient dog peeking into the shop with eyes almost as dark as Lisa's. Half covered in mud, a rough rope tied around his neck, he looked miserable.

And that got Gray pissed really quick.

Breathing hard behind him, unaware of the dog, Lisa whispered, "Oh, God."

"Shh," he told her. "It's a stray dog."

Immediately her head popped up over his shoulder. "Ohhh," she whispered. "The poor baby. Is he hurt?"

"I don't know, but he's not in good shape." Hearing them, the animal started to slink away, so Gray said to her, "Stay here."

"What are you going to do?"

"Check on him, if I can." Help him, if at all possible. "C'mere, boy. You okay? Scared, huh. I bet." He kept his voice low and made painstaking progress at getting closer. The rope around the animal's neck looked too damned tight, like a cruel trick. He'd seen a lot of shit in his lifetime, but anything involving animals or kids really did him in.

He heard Lisa moving behind him, and a second later he felt her touch on his back. "Offer him this."

He took the beef jerky and held it out.

The dog went on alert, ears up, nose sniffing the air.

Chances of getting bitten seemed good, so Gray tossed a piece toward the dog.

He caught it in the air and swallowed it in one gulp.

Yeah, that rope dug into the dog's neck, way too tight. Gray tossed another bite, making this one closer so the dog had to step farther inside while Gray circled to the side. He kept it up, wanting to get behind the dog so he could close the door.

But first... "Lisa, I need you to go up to my place. If the dog freaks out, I don't want you to get bit."

"No."

Since he'd given that order in his best cop voice, he stalled. "This isn't—"

"Hush, Gray." Phone to her ear, she said, "Hey, Dad, it's me. We need a little bit of help. I don't suppose you have any free time?" Quickly she explained the situation, and when she disconnected, she said, "He's on his way."

What the hell? Did she think her dad could do something he couldn't?

"He's a vet," she reminded him. "And we're in luck. He was using today for house calls, so he's not that far away. Fifteen minutes, he said. Instead of trying to trap the dog, let's just keep feeding him. Once he's here, Dad will know what to do."

It wasn't in Gray's nature to ask for help, but Lisa seemed to have no problem with it. At least when the help came from her family.

"All right," Gray agreed. "Find some more food. But I don't want you near him."

Instead of taking exception to that, she said, "Gray? Is that a note tied to the dog's neck?"

He'd already seen it, so he only nodded. "Yeah." And far as he was concerned, whoever had put it there needed his ass kicked.

## *CHAPTER SIX*

HER DAD GOT there in under ten minutes, and he had both Uncle Sawyer and Nadine, Shohn's fiancée, with him.

As her dad worked his magic, talking soothingly to the dog and quickly earning his trust, Lisa whispered, "Nadine owns a pet hotel, so she's really great with animals, too."

Beside them, arms crossed as he watched, her uncle Sawyer said, "Jordan has a way with animals."

Gray looked impressed. "He whispered and the dog just came to him. Like he knew him or something."

"They all do that with Dad."

Nadine nodded. "I've seen him whisper to cows and goats and hawks and groundhogs. They all love him."

The exaggeration, slight as it might be, made Lisa grin, especially since it looked as though Gray believed her. Her grin died, however, once the rope was off the dog and they saw the note.

Jordan handed it off to Nadine, who read it and then handed it to Sawyer. "'*You'll pay,*'" he read. And then to Gray, "Any ideas?"

"Yeah. A cruel idiot." Seeing Jordan had it under control, Gray joined him, going down on his haunches to cautiously stroke the marks left around the dog's throat. "He'll be okay?"

"She, but yes."

"She?"

Lisa grinned again at Gray's expression. "A girl, Dad?"

"Yes, and by the looks of her, I'd say she's at least twelve, maybe older. A mutt, but I see a lot of coonhound in her. She's malnourished, has some small wounds that need attention, and she needs a good cleaning." He looked at Gray. "If it's okay with you, I'd like to take her in and get her treated."

"Please," Gray said. "Do whatever she needs and then let me know what I owe you." He again stroked the dog, and this time she tipped her head up, her eyes closed as if relishing the touch.

Lisa understood that; she often felt the same when Gray put those warm, strong hands on her.

Nadine nudged her, and she realized both her dad and Uncle Sawyer were watching her. Clearing her throat, she asked Gray, "Do you plan to keep her?"

"Yes."

No hesitation. She really liked that about him. Decisive. Caring. "I'm glad."

Her dad got a crate from the back of his truck. "If I'd known I'd be bringing one back with me," he said, "I'd have lined it with something soft."

"Here." Just like that, Gray pulled off his T-shirt and handed it over.

Neither her dad nor her uncle seemed to think anything of it, but once Lisa got her eyes to blink she noticed that Nadine was staring with rapt surprise.

It was Lisa's turn to offer a nudge.

Nadine turned to her and silently mouthed, *Wow*.

Nodding, Lisa agreed with her.

"I understand she'll be fine with you," Gray was saying to her dad. "But I feel bad just letting her go."

"Then don't." Uncle Sawyer, avoiding her gaze, stepped in. "Sheriff Turley's going to need to see that note."

"I'll handle it," Gray said with silky menace.

"All the same, Turley needs to know. I'm free today, Jordan's free, and I'm sure Lisa can handle the shop for a few hours."

Seeing a trap closing in, Lisa said, "But—"

"Ride back with us," Sawyer continued. "After we talk to the sheriff, I can show you Jordan's clinic. It'll give us a chance to get better acquainted."

Her dad gave her a look, then said to Gray, "We'll need to fill out some paperwork for her. On the way to the clinic, you can think up a name."

The dog, after sniffing the shirt Jordan spread in the crate, went in willingly.

"She's smart," Nadine said. "If there's anything you need from me, let me know. Otherwise I think I'll hang out and give Lisa a hand."

Again, Lisa tried to protest.

But Gray beat her to the punch, asking, "Do you mind?" His eyes, the color of the stormy sky, stared into hers. "I'll be back before we're due to close."

He might as well have said, *In time to give you everything I promised with that hot, killer kiss.*

The dog watched her, so how could she refuse? Deflated, Lisa flapped a hand. "It's been a slow day, what with the rain. Go on. I'm sure we'll be fine."

Grinning, probably anticipating a lot of girl talk, Nadine said, "This is going to be fun."

Gray said, "Let me grab another shirt and I'll be right with you." He disappeared inside.

Lisa stood there, her father, uncle and Nadine all

watching her. She chose to focus on the dog. "Such a sweetie. How long will you need to keep her?"

"If there's nothing major wrong, I can give her back to you at the picnic Sunday."

"Back to Gray, you mean."

Her dad just gave her another long look.

Luckily Gray returned, still buttoning up his short-sleeved cotton shirt. He paused beside her, said, "I won't be long," and right there, in front of family and a friend, he put his mouth to hers.

Lisa was so shocked she didn't even blink.

Smiling, he touched her cheek. "You have my number if anything comes up." He kissed her again, then strode to the dog crate and, like freaking Superman, put his hand in the handle and lifted it as if it didn't hold a large dog.

Sawyer grinned back at Lisa. "I like him."

Brows up, her dad opened the back of the truck. "Yeah."

When Gray said, "I'll ride back here with her," Nadine put a hand to her heart and whispered, "Oh, me, too."

Amazing. Gray had told her he could handle her family. She'd had her doubts, but wow, he'd just made it look pretty easy.

They were all won over.

And if she were honest with herself, she'd admit she wasn't far behind them.

TUCKER TURLEY DIDN'T like the note, or the treatment of the dog, any more than Gray had, but as he'd already known, a note wasn't much to go on.

"Could've been meant for anyone," the sheriff said.

"Yeah," Gray agreed. But he trusted gut instincts,

and his gut said the dog had been sent to him, specifically.

Which meant the lame *You'll pay* was a direct threat. So someone had a beef with him? He'd gotten along fine with all the locals, so he didn't have a clue.

They left with Tucker promising he'd keep both an eye and ear out. Neither Sawyer nor Jordan looked happy. And he knew why.

After they reached the clinic, Gray hovered nearby while Jordan checked the dog from nose to tail. He gave her some pain meds that he said would also make her sleepy. He put ointment on the raw abrasions on her neck, cleaned out her ears, checked her teeth and decided to let her eat and get a good night's sleep before bathing her in the morning.

After all that, they got the dog settled in a roomy kennel area, and Jordan said, "Let's get some coffee in the break room."

Which Gray knew was a euphemism for *Let us grill you to our satisfaction.*

He started the conversation by saying, "Hell of a nice setup you have."

"Thanks." Jordan filled three disposable cups, then pulled out a seat and sank into it. "Any thoughts on a name?"

"Yeah." Gray sipped his coffee, knew the men were analyzing him and said, "Shelby."

"Interesting choice," Sawyer said.

Shrugging, Gray explained, "My deceased partner's last name."

Clearly they already knew his background, given their quiet nods of respect. After a stretch of time, Jordan set his coffee aside. "Are you going to convince my daughter to stay in Buckhorn?"

Gray didn't deny that they had a relationship beyond employer and employee. Neither of these men was blind or stupid.

And of course, they'd witnessed the very deliberate, possessive kiss he'd given her.

But he wouldn't mind using the opportunity to get a point across. "I don't want to pressure her. All of you are doing enough of that."

Sawyer and Jordan shared a frown.

"What I will do," Gray said, "is give her plenty of reasons to stay."

The frowns smoothed out and the men grinned. As if remembering himself, Jordan coughed his away. "Lisa is—"

"Very special. I know."

Jordan agreed. "She's smart, and she can take care of herself. But if you have some nutcase after you, is it safe?"

"You don't have to worry." Gray knew well the dangers that existed in the world. "Whatever the note meant, no matter what the threat might be, I won't let anything happen to her."

After quietly taking that in, Sawyer asked, "You're armed?"

"At the shop, yes. Going forward, I will be everywhere." He hoped they understood that for a cop, carrying was second nature. "But even without a gun, I'd protect her."

Sawyer smiled. "Even though he's mayor now, Morgan says he feels naked without his gun."

"True story." Gray liked the familiar feel of the

weapon, whether in a hip holster or at the small of his back. "Once a cop, always a cop."

Jordan said, "He told us about your partner. That had to be tough."

Sawyer tipped his head, his attention on Gray's leg. "You're okay now? Have full mobility back?"

"I'm fine." Gray saw the questions they didn't ask. Might as well clear the air now. He spent the next hour or so talking, and in the process he learned that he liked Sawyer and Jordan both. They were interested without being overly intrusive. Protective of Lisa while also showing their respect and insisting they trusted her to make the decisions best for her.

As a doctor, Sawyer asked plenty of questions about Gray's injury. Jordan had a quieter way about him, but Gray thought it might be deceptive, a way to hide the intensity.

They were good men, and he was glad Lisa had them in her life.

Before they left the clinic, Gray again checked on Shelby. Now that she'd been fed and had some meds, she was resting peacefully on a plush doggy bed—and his shirt. He stroked her, enjoyed the thumping of her tail and promised her he'd see her again in the morning. She closed her eyes on a big doggy yawn, so Gray didn't linger.

The later it got, the fewer people would be at the marina and the better the chance of Lisa being alone.

By the time Jordan dropped Gray back at the shop, it was raining again. Thanks to a call, they knew Nadine had left half an hour ago because business was so slow. Gray saw a man using the ramp to take a boat out. Along the shore, only two people, a woman and a man, cast out lines, their hats and windbreakers the only sign that they noticed the weather.

"Thanks again," Gray said to Jordan.

"You know, the previous owners sometimes closed up early on days like this. You could do the same."

Seeing Lisa in the doorway waiting on him, Gray decided that wasn't a bad idea. "Sounds like a plan." He opened the door and stepped into the downpour.

"Gray?"

He ducked his head back into the open truck door.

"Don't make me regret liking you."

Grinning, Gray closed the door and jogged to the shop. Soon as he reached the door, Lisa stepped back. She looked both worried and anxious and, damn, he wanted her.

Standing there, dripping on the floor, Gray looked her over. There seemed to be a sort of leashed tension in her small body. He saw her hands shaking, the shallow way she breathed. "Any problems?"

"No."

Hoping for the best, he asked, "Miss me?"

"Yes."

He drew a breath and went for broke. "I want you, Lisa. Right now."

As if that galvanized her, she rushed to the door, slammed and locked it.

Gray watched her, his heart racing, already getting hard.

Shooting to the window next, she turned the Open sign to Closed, then pulled the curtains so no one could see in.

"In a hurry?" he asked, so turned on he couldn't draw a deep breath.

"Yes." She headed past him for the door to the stairs. "Come on."

Snagging her hand as she passed, Gray pulled her back. "Just a second." Suffering his own urgency, he got his gun and keys from a drawer beneath the counter. Lisa didn't balk at the gun. She didn't even look all that surprised by it.

Stepping back, she let him unlock the stairs door and, after he relocked it with them on the other side, followed him at a more sedate pace up to his living area. Once there, Gray put the gun and keys on the table in the small kitchen, then stripped off his soaked shirt and draped it over a chair.

Lisa made a sound, stepped up against him, her hands on his chest, and a second later she went to her tiptoes to kiss him.

No longer caring that he was soaked through, Gray gathered her closer, his hands going down her slim back, cupping under her bottom, the backs of her thighs, back up again. Her hands were the same, sliding down his back to his shorts, then back up to curve over his shoulders.

He felt the sting of her nails and she practically tried to crawl into him.

He pressed her back enough to get the buttons on her blouse open, but he needed to kiss her, too, and soon they were tangled again. Once he got the top buttons undone, he managed to pull the blouse up and over her head.

No bra.

Breathing hard, he held her back and looked at her.

The frayed cutoffs fit low on her hips, showing off the slight curve of her belly, the dip of her waist, all that smooth, soft, pale peach skin. The shorts, faded and worn in spots, were about the sexiest thing he'd ever seen on a woman.

On this woman, they all but destroyed him.

Traveling upward, his hungry gaze took in her round, firm breasts. Excitement had drawn her nipples tight. His lungs constricted, his hands naturally lifting to cover her, to tease those stiffened nipples with his thumbs. A groan rumbled from deep in his chest.

At the same time, Lisa purred, her hands covering his.

"You're as beautiful as I remember."

When she started to kiss him, he whispered, "I want to see all of you," and reluctantly pulled his hands away. Taking a step back, he reached for the snap of her shorts. It opened easily and, taunting himself and her, he slowly dragged down the zipper.

Lisa stood there shivering with need, her attention on his face, seeing everything he felt. And he felt a lot.

With her shorts open, he put both hands inside the back, cuddling her cheeks for a moment and then sliding both her panties and her shorts down. Once past her thighs they dropped to her feet.

So sweet. And so fucking pretty. All over.

"Gray?"

He smoothed her hair behind her shoulders and just looked at her. He could look at her for a lifetime. He knew it, had felt it almost from the moment they'd met. She was his, now and always. The trick would be in getting her to want the same thing.

"Your turn," she said, lifting one hand to tease at the drawstrings to his shorts.

"No problem." He shucked off his remaining clothes

in record time, then made her squeal when he scooped her up and headed for his bedroom. "Kiss me."

She did, and damn, but her kisses were hotter than sex with other women. She scorched him, especially with the hot way her tongue played with his, how her bare breasts felt on his chest, the way her fingers dug into his shoulders as she tried to hold him tighter.

At the side of the bed, he sank down with her small body tucked under his. She slid one leg up and around his hip, both her hands easing up to tangle in his hair while they indulged in a deep, eating kiss that left each of them panting.

Needing more, Gray nibbled a damp path down her throat to her breasts. He already knew she had extremely sensitive nipples, and he loved it. He started with a few licks, then sucked on her until she groaned. Carefully, he caught her pebbled nipple in his teeth and tugged.

*"Gray."*

Taking turns at each breast, he enjoyed her until she was crying out, her head back, her body moving rhythmically against his.

Wanting to see her come, he stroked a hand down her side, over that cute belly and between her legs, where he found her hot and already wet.

"Yeah," he rasped low, slicking his fingers over her, then in her to press deep.

She said his name on a high, thin cry.

Watching her, he brought his fingers out, up to her clitoris, then back in, pumping two or three times, then teasing her clit again. Over and over. She found his rhythm, her hips rolling, her throaty groans coming faster.

He licked over her already wet nipples, sucked insistently, and far too soon she started coming.

Gray held her, stayed with her, wrung her out until her hoarse cries faded and she went limp on the bed, eyes closed, lips parted.

Seeing her like that, sated by him, left protective, possessive urges surging through him. Even knowing it was too soon, he wanted to declare himself. Time wouldn't change anything for him, but hopefully it would for her.

Odd, but now that he had her here in his bed, he no longer felt the churning rush to get inside her. Instead he took immense pleasure in cuddling her, kissing her, touching her in soft, easy strokes over her waist, her shoulder, along her hip and thigh.

After a time, she sighed deeply, smiled a little. "I needed that."

"Mmm." He nuzzled her shoulder, breathed in her scrumptious scent and took a lazy bite. "Me, too."

With a husky laugh, she pressed at his chest. "That took the edge off, but I need more."

"A lot more." Sitting up, he snagged a condom from the bottom drawer of the nightstand. As he rolled it on, he felt her hand on his back, idly touching him. He turned, kneed her legs apart and settled over her. "Hi."

Her eyes, all warm, dark and mysterious, smiled at him. "Hi."

Adjusting, he moved against her, watched her face and sank in.

"Gray," she moaned.

Doing his utmost to maintain control, he began rocking into her, deeper each time, until their bodies were in perfect tune. It was all familiar, irresistible and yet still new because now he knew her, really knew her. And loved everything about her. "I enjoy hearing you say my name."

Opening her eyes and staring up at him, she whispered, "Gray."

"Tease." Her body squeezed around his cock, wetter and hotter. Ducking his face into her neck, he opened his mouth against her fragrant skin.

"I like teasing you." Her legs lifted around him and she locked her ankles at the small of his back. Near his ear she whispered, "Harder." And as he complied, she lifted into him, saying again, *"Gray."*

Damn. Her teeth caught his shoulder, she cried out, and this time, unable to stop himself, Gray came with her.

Sometime later he became aware of Lisa toying with his chest hair. He hugged her, kissed her forehead and rolled to his back.

She immediately moved over him.

Liking that, he murmured, "Nice."

"I don't want you to get too far away."

"Yeah?" Smiling, feeling more relaxed than he had in…well, a month, he settled a hand on her bottom. "Stay over and I promise to keep you within touching distance all night long."

Surprise widened her eyes, then she flushed. "I wasn't hinting."

"I know. I want you here." More than that, he *needed* her close. "Stay."

For only a moment she thought about it. "Okay." As she snuggled in, she said, "It'll give us a chance to talk."

Biting back his groan wasn't easy, but Gray managed it and even sounded casual when he asked, "Talk about what?"

She rose up to her elbows. "You. Your partner." Her hand went down his body to the top of his thigh—dangerously close to his junk—and settled over the scar. "And how you got this."

## *CHAPTER SEVEN*

TEN MINUTES LATER, Lisa found herself sitting at Gray's kitchen table wearing one of his shirts and nothing else while he walked around in snug boxers and nothing else, making them sandwiches.

"I named the dog Shelby, after my partner, Vic Shelby."

Lisa sipped a glass of sweet tea and watched Gray. Just looking at him was wonderful. Long, leanly muscled thighs sprinkled with dark hair. Flat abs sporting that incredibly sexy happy trail. And his chest and shoulders...

Looking at him melted her bones and made her skin too tight and stirred that insanely hot, sweet lust to life again.

It swelled her heart to know he would finally open up to her, and the combo of lust and tenderness nearly did her in.

"I like the name."

"Good, because I'm keeping Shelby. I'd planned to get a dog after I got settled in anyway. She's such a sweetheart, and some coward used her to send me that note."

"And keeping her is the least you can do because you feel responsible?"

Turning his back to her as he sliced a tomato, he lifted a shoulder. "That covers it."

His back was as amazing as the rest of him. And that tight butt...but it was his big heart that really got to her. "Aww."

He scoffed at that. "Like I said, I wanted a dog anyway." He glanced back at her. "You don't mind?"

"One thing you should know about my family, we're very pet friendly. I didn't have a dog or cat because I traveled all the time. But I love animals."

"And now that you're here?"

She knew he deliberately left that open-ended. Unlike everyone else in her life right now, Gray didn't push. He made his intentions known, and he was real up-front about wanting her. But that was as far as he took it. She appreciated that a lot. "Now that I'm here, I'd be happy to help with Shelby." And maybe, if she ended up staying, she'd get a dog, too, a companion for Shelby. Or maybe a cat. She'd have to think about it.

"Now, about you and your partner and that wound that nearly unmanned you?"

"It was close, but luckily missed the vital parts."

Very close. The scar, a jagged line, cut across the top of one thigh. Healed now, thank God, but what if it had been a few inches over? Worse, what if it had been a killing blow?

Gray studied her, then went back to the sandwich prep. "So one day Shelby—my partner—and I were checking out a domestic dispute. A neighbor had called about the noise, said she heard a lot of angry arguing. From the second we got there, I knew it was going to be bad. There were three men and one woman and tensions were already so high, no one was listening.

Some scumbag had hit his wife, and her two brothers were there to defend her. The husband and one of the brothers had felony records, everyone was ramped up on adrenaline and rage, and before we could even ask any questions, shit went south in a big way."

Gray had stopped moving. He had a butter knife in one hand, a piece of bread in the other, but he just… stood there. He seemed lost in the memory. A very ugly memory, given the strain in his broad shoulders.

Leaving her seat, Lisa walked over to him. She gently took the butter knife and bread and finished spreading the mayonnaise. "That's when you got hit?"

He pinched the bridge of his nose and put his head down. "Shelby took one to the chest and went down fast. I tried to cover him, but it felt like everyone was shooting, me, the two brothers, the husband…"

She leaned into him but didn't look right at him. She sensed how personal and painful this still was for him. "I can't imagine how devastating that must've been."

"We're trained," he said. "But there'd been no prior indication we were walking into a fucking war zone. The entire time we were shooting, the lady screamed—until she wasn't anymore."

Hurting for him, Lisa swallowed hard, tears clogging her throat.

"I was crouched over Shelby, covering him the best I could, and I got off some good shots. Hit one of the brothers and her husband, but the other dude ran off. The woman was already dead. Blood was literally everywhere, soaking Shelby, all over me…"

Suddenly he caught himself. She heard him taking deep breaths, saw his hands clench and unclench. After a low, nearly inaudible curse, he turned and leaned on the counter, watching her.

Lisa did her best to look…not devastated. But in her mind she saw it all and her heart wept for him. In a very short time, he'd come to mean a great deal to her. She couldn't bear the thought of him hurting, and yet he'd almost died.

Quietly, she finished the sandwiches and cut them into halves.

"You're pretty good at this," he finally said.

The lump in her throat almost strangled her, but she managed to keep things light. "At finishing up almost-finished sandwiches?"

"At listening." His warm, somber gaze went over her. "And looking good while doing it."

She gestured at his shirt, which she wore. "What? This old thing? I just threw it on."

Smiling, Gray pulled her in close for a kiss and then just held her, his arms around her, his chin on the top of her head.

"You're okay?"

"Yeah." He squeezed her. "The bullet to my thigh just grazed me. At the time I didn't even feel it. It wasn't until the paramedics showed up and told me I'd been hit that it started to hurt like a son of a bitch." He quieted, and Lisa waited, her arms around him, her cheek to his chest, listening to the steady thump of his heart. "The woman and one of her brothers were dead. Her husband, wounded, didn't put up much resistance after that. They found her other brother within ten minutes."

"Your partner was already gone?"

"No." Gray's hands contracted on her. "He held

on for three long weeks. Seeing his wife go through that—I think that might've been the hardest part. We all knew he wouldn't make it, that we were leaning on false hope. But you can't help yourself."

"No."

"I'd just left the funeral when I met you."

She kissed his bare chest, then his shoulder, then went on tiptoe to reach his chin and finally his mouth. "I'm very, very glad you survived, Gray Neely."

Smoothing back her hair, looking at her, really looking at her, Gray nodded. "Me, too. Though I spent a hell of a lot of time wallowing in guilt because of it."

"I wish you wouldn't."

"That's the thing." He cupped her face, his expression serious. "I waffled between guilt and rage and being just plain numb. I wasn't sure what I wanted to do, or where I wanted to do it. But that night with you, I finally *felt* again. Everything. All good stuff. I thought I'd never see you again, and I hated that, but I woke that next morning knowing I would start fresh."

"In Buckhorn."

"Random shot in the dark, babe. I was checking around for something different and saw the ad for the marina."

"That's certainly different."

"But you know what?"

Since he was smiling now, Lisa smiled, too. "What?"

"I think it was fate." Scooping his hands under her bottom, he lifted her up and stepped to the wall, gently pinning her in place. His voice went husky and his lips almost touched hers. "I think we're good together."

Though she told herself that her plans were still up in the air, her heart tried to dance out of her chest. "I think so, too." Until Gray, sex was something she could take or leave, and usually she left it in favor of other, more exciting things—like wrapping up a new deal or finishing a business project. Now, well, she was starving but she'd gladly forgo the sandwiches if he wanted to take her right now. She couldn't imagine anything that could take her away.

In that moment, there was nothing she wanted more than Gray.

And from the look in his eyes, she thought he might be feeling the same.

"No pressure," he whispered. "I want you. Just about every way there is."

Wait—*what was he saying?*

"But if you decided tomorrow to go back to your old job, I'd still be here in Buckhorn."

"Um…okay?"

He smiled. "I want you to understand. You don't need to feel responsible for what we do or don't do, or how it might turn out. I like it here. I like your family, seeing the people who fish or swim or ski, the rowdy kids everywhere, and I like the lake. The broiling sunshine. The damp wind. All the birds and the frogs and turtles. All of it. I'm guessing I'll even like the winter, when everything is frozen and white and I'll be able to loaf around and put my feet up."

It wasn't easy to think because, really, he'd pinned her with his hips, which meant she felt his very noticeable erection. And he'd said he wanted her in *every way there is*. Confusing, to say the least—like, did he mean he wanted her beyond the physical, or maybe long-term?

All that, along with the scent of his warm body and

the way he watched her with those stormy gray eyes—well, none of it was conducive to clear thought.

So she nodded.

That made his smile widen. "You have enough pressure, honey. You won't get it from me. Know that I want you, but if you want something different, I'll deal with it. That's all I'm saying."

Instead of giving her a chance to come up with a reply, or even to decide how she felt about his blithe attitude, he leaned in for a kiss, warm and soft, moving over her lips until she sighed. And maybe squirmed against him a little.

Her thoughts dissolved, her only focus on his mouth and how he tasted and how perfectly he worked those deliciously sculpted lips against hers. But as he started to trail kisses down her throat, she thought of something he'd said. "Wait."

"Okay."

She gasped for air, shook her head to clear the fog and caught his intent expression. "So." One more necessary breath and she felt clearer minded. "You plan to take the winters off?"

"Shocking idea for you, huh?" He kissed the end of her nose, as if her astonishment was...cute. "I like the idea of working hard all summer, relaxing during the worst months in the winter. I'm thinking spring and fall will still bring in some business, right?"

Could he afford to just take off for months at a time? How much did cops make anyway? Surely not—

As if he'd read her mind, he put his forehead to hers. "I bought the house and business outright. I'm thirty-two and single, and I was always frugal, so I had decent savings. Add that to the profit I made when I sold my house, which had been a fixer-upper, and it was easy enough. All I'm paying on is my boat."

Lisa sifted through everything he'd said, wondering why he'd told her about his financial status. But mostly she focused on one particular thing. She pushed him back to see him. "You have a boat?"

"You haven't noticed it sitting out back?" Mouth twisting, he added, "Still on a trailer?"

Of course she'd seen it, but...there were a lot of boats sitting around the lot. In fact, that was probably partial income in the winter, storing boats in a secure place. "You have a boat."

"Fishing poles, too." He shrugged. "Seemed necessary, with me buying a marina and all."

"A boat." Why hadn't she realized? "Well, we need to put it in."

Very slowly, he grinned, then nudged his erection at her. "With you so far."

Her face went hot. "Not *that*." What was she saying? Backtracking, she corrected, "Okay, that, too." He leaned in for another kiss, but she dodged him this time. "I meant your boat. Have you been out on the lake?"

"Once, before I bought this place." He got comfortable—pressed tight to her. "The previous owner took me around."

She gave it some thought. "How many hours do you plan to give to Petie?"

Gray shrugged, and as usual she enjoyed the flex of his strong shoulders. He held her up, between the wall and his body, with ease. "Now that he's back for the rest of the season, I was thinking a few hours each evening, Monday through Thursday, then half a day on Sunday."

"Perfect." She could work with that. "What about me?"

He put soft, damp bites on her neck. "When I get off, I want you to get off."

The toe-curling way he teased distracted her, but to be sure, she asked, "Are we talking about work?"

"That, too." Grinning, he lifted his head and kissed her mouth. "I want us to have a few evenings together, and Sunday afternoons, too."

He'd already been thinking about it? Planning for more time with her? That deserved a big hug, which she gave him. "You're an excellent planner."

"Know what I'm planning now?"

Her heart skipped a beat and she whispered, "Tell me."

"I'm planning to eat a sandwich."

"Gray!"

He smooched her again. "With you." Slowly he lowered her to her feet. "Then a shower."

She frowned.

Until he said, "With you."

Now that sounded better.

"And then I want to go back to bed—"

"With me?"

He nodded. "And I'm going to love you head to toes, and all those hot places in between, until you give me some of those sexy moans and sighs again, and then I'm going to hold you all night. What do you think?"

Lisa smiled dreamily. "Sounds like the perfect plan to me."

SHELBY CAME HOME midmorning the next day. Jordan delivered her, then hung around a few minutes to ensure she was comfortable and to go over some meds with Gray.

Looking very uncertain, the dog sniffed around, wary of everyone but hungry for affection. Gray admired her now, after her bath and with her fur brushed. "She's beautiful."

"Mostly a bluetick coonhound," Jordan said, "but a mix for sure. Smart and gentle. I'm guessing at least ten years old, maybe older. I don't think she's at all aggressive, but keep an eye on her, okay?"

"I'm sure we'll get along just fine." Gray was careful to stroke her gently, especially around her abraded neck, taking care not to move too fast.

The rest of the day Shelby mostly slept, and the day after that she ate and slept, and the day after that she strolled out to the docks to laze in the sun—until kids showed up, then she lazed inside...and slept.

From what he could tell she didn't have a single aggressive bone in her body. If anything, she was too timid. But at her age, and having been neglected, it made sense that she might be uncertain.

Every so often, if Gray sat long enough, Shelby would come over and stare at him, then lean on his leg. He quickly learned that was his cue to pet or scratch or just give affection. She'd tip up her face, close her eyes, and it looked as though she smiled.

She showed no interest in getting on the furniture and chose to sleep alone at night, which was a good thing since she snored. Loudly.

The first time he heard it was only a few hours after he'd made love with Lisa. They both should have been sleeping, but the noise kept him awake. He'd come up on an elbow to look at Lisa.

Eyes open, she said, "Don't even think to blame me."

He grinned. "It's the dog."

"Yeah." Lisa smiled, too. She'd fallen fast and hard for Shelby, and did her best to pamper the dog. For the most part Shelby let her. "Guess we should get used to it."

That simple statement had affected Gray, because it was an indication that she planned to stick around. And thinking that stirred him, so it was an hour later before they got back to sleep. And he'd held Lisa close all night.

Each and every night, Lisa stayed over. She always wanted him to talk, so he did, but she didn't enjoy sharing about herself. She especially didn't want to talk about her job or whether or not she'd be staying in Buckhorn. So he didn't ask.

Everything he learned about her was from experiencing her, and paying close attention. Not a problem, since Lisa fascinated him.

When it came to Shelby, she seemed to have a sixth sense and just knew when the dog needed her. Like the time a woman came in with her little snapping dog that yapped incessantly and had Shelby backed up with her scruff starting to rise.

Suddenly Lisa was there, kneeling by Shelby, soothing her while glaring daggers at the lady. Gray scooped up her little ankle biter, got bitten in the process and nicely requested that the woman keep the dog on a leash, or carry it.

It wasn't until the lady was leaving that he found out she was single—since she asked him out.

That was also when he got reminded of Lisa's temper.

Gray had only smiled and thanked the woman,

ready to make his excuses, when Lisa said, "Honey, did you want to grill tonight?" And she'd pulled him down to kiss him. On the mouth. *Deliberately* for the lady... who left with an apologetic smile, carrying her dog.

Yup, Lisa had a temper, as he'd witnessed when that yahoo had thrown the kid in the lake. Gray would never forget seeing the guy shout back at her and how he'd wanted to take the man apart.

But in most cases Lisa had great control and even better tact. Overall the customers, visitors and locals alike, loved her.

Some of the hopefuls that Amber had originally brought around still tried to flirt, but she was never more than casually friendly. He respected that a lot.

Lisa didn't need compliments to continually feed her ego. She was smart, talented and accomplished. She knew it but didn't brag about it.

Every damn day he wondered if she could possibly be content in Buckhorn. She didn't seem bored. But neither did she say the menial work fulfilled her.

Shelby loved her. If she didn't stick around, the dog would miss her horribly. In fact, Shelby fretted every morning when Lisa insisted on driving home to jog—for appearances.

Gray didn't tell her that she'd seriously underestimated the intelligence of her family if she thought they hadn't yet figured it out. From what he could tell, they were all observant enough to understand the way of things. Hell, Gray didn't want to hide it.

But apparently Lisa did. So every morning she drove home and jogged and then came back to work with him wearing fresh clothes.

If he had his way he'd just move her in, but her

house was nice enough that he supposed that didn't make sense to her.

On the morning of the picnic, as Lisa was preparing to go, Gray walked Shelby downstairs to let her out in the back lot where she usually did her business. She still navigated the stairs with no problem, but at ten, how much longer could that last? Something to think about.

The stairs opened into the shop, and Gray immediately sensed something was wrong. Setting aside his coffee cup, he looked around but saw nothing amiss. Shelby, picking up on his tension or maybe sensing something he didn't, gave a low snarl and crept toward the door that would lead to the back lot.

The dog was normally so passive that the feral sound surprised Gray.

"Easy." He put a hand in her collar in case he needed to restrain her, then opened the door—and stepped into one hell of a mess.

Shelby tried to dart out, but he stopped her. Until he made sure the vandal was gone, he wouldn't take any chances. Turning, he called toward the stairs, "Lisa? I need you."

LISA STOOD BACK with Shelby on her leash, distraught over the destruction done to the lot. Shelby wasn't happy, either, so on top of taking it all in, Lisa did her best to soothe the dog.

Splattered paint covered everything, thrown on the trees and Shelby's new fence and the grass. Vile words covered the back of the building and the trailer for Gray's boat.

His boat.

*Oh, no.* Pivoting around, urging Shelby to follow, Lisa started down to the docks.

Gray materialized in front of her. He looked scruffy, intense and all alpha-male protective. "Where are you going?"

Lisa had a hard time answering. Gray hadn't yet put on a shirt or shoes, and his shorts hung low. She knew he tried to keep his expression neutral. Did he fear showing her the anger he surely had to feel?

How had he even noticed her leaving? One moment he'd been talking with Tucker and Morgan, who'd again shown up together. They'd been calculating the damage, going over everything, and then poof, Gray stood there in front of her.

Lisa shifted her bare feet on the dew-wet grass. The sun was up, already scorching the day, but night on the lake always left everything wet with humidity. It'd take another hour at least to dry out the area. "Your trailer is ruined."

"It can be cleaned off, probably with a power washer."

"It can?"

He scratched his bare chest, swatted away a bee and stared down at her. "Wet as everything is, the paint didn't get a good chance to dry. It'll be fine." He dropped his hands back to his hips and asked again, "Where are you headed?"

She hated to say it aloud, but he waited, his gaze never wavering from hers... She winced. "Your boat."

His face went blank before dark emotion flashed into his stormy eyes. "Shit." He took off at a fast clip down to the shore, striding along the boardwalk and then down the dock and—she heard his muttered curse over whatever he found.

He'd been through so much, but he'd found his place again here. He liked Buckhorn. Really liked it. *Why was someone tormenting him like this?*

Coming up alongside her, Morgan automatically reached for the leash and took the dog from her. Shelby didn't mind. She panted up at Morgan with near adoration. Her uncle, a big softie when it came to animals, squatted down to give the dog attention.

Shelby sniffed him all over.

"She smells your own pets," Lisa told him. Shelby had an amazing nose. Often she'd smell a dog before customers entered with their pets.

"You're a good girl, aren't you?" Morgan said to Shelby, then he looked up at Lisa. "He's made an enemy."

The sudden switch threw her. "Gray? Don't be silly. Everyone loves him."

His brow went up. "Everyone, huh?"

She froze, but quickly shook it off. "With the security lights and knowing Gray lived upstairs, a person would have to be very ballsy to get close enough to do all this."

"Ballsy, or nuts," Morgan said, standing again. "I'm betting on both."

"That's why you're here?"

He shrugged. "Tucker told me when Gray called. Assuming you'd be here, too, I decided to tag along."

Lisa snorted. Morgan might have retired as the sheriff, but he still involved himself in every situation.

"Know what I'm wondering?"

Feeling a trap, Lisa didn't look at him. But that didn't stop her uncle Morgan. Very little ever did.

"I'm wondering why Gray didn't hear anything. He must have been...preoccupied?"

"Or sleeping," she said with a frown. "Don't most people sleep at night?"

"Yeah." Morgan still watched her too closely. "Unless someone is fresh to a romance. Then there are usually better things to be doing, things that could distract a man."

So now she was a distraction?

The sounds of a truck on the gravel drive saved her from replying. Both she and Morgan turned to see Garrett had arrived. Her cousin, Morgan's son, was a firefighter. He was also friends with Tucker. For those reasons, Lisa supposed he had some interest in any mischief caused in Buckhorn.

Looking around again, she took mental inventory of what would be needed to clean and repair everything.

"So you spent the night, huh?"

Startled by that abrupt statement, her gaze clashed with her uncle's again. Her laugh sounded guilty, as did her exclaimed *"What?"*

Morgan looked at the dog, shook his head as if Shelby would understand and then slung an arm around her. "I know the signs, honey, so don't bother denying it. I'm not judging you. I'm just surprised. I mean, that was fast."

Heat rushed into her face. What would Morgan think if he knew she'd originally hooked up with Gray within hours of meeting him?

"Never known you to move fast before."

"Uncle Morgan—"

"I've never known her to move at all," Garrett said, joining them. "She's usually too involved with her work. But Gray seems all right."

They heard Gray muttering curses mixed with threats as he pulled ruined equipment out of his boat.

"All things considered," Morgan said.

"If he coerces her into staying," Garrett added, "then I like him."

"He's not coercing," her dad said, making Lisa jump. "Told me so himself."

Lisa rounded on him, and saw that he had her uncle Sawyer and Shohn with him.

Shohn said, "Hey, cuz," as if they hadn't already intruded.

She threw up her hands. "This is ridiculous. It was vandalism. Why are you all congregating here?"

Sawyer drew her away from Morgan and in for a hug. "Because you're here."

"That's what I told her," Morgan said.

"And Gray," Shohn added, "has an enemy."

"Told her that, too."

"No one wants you caught up in this," her dad told her.

Damn her fair skin, she blushed from her neck to her hairline, and no wonder, with the majority of her male relatives standing there studying her, knowing her and making some accurate guesses.

As her dad searched her face, his brows shot up. He glanced at Morgan, who shrugged. Then at Garrett, who grinned.

Shohn sighed. "Well, hell. You're already in it knee-deep, aren't you?"

## *CHAPTER EIGHT*

THAT PARTICULAR SUNDAY, the family picnic got moved to the marina. With Lisa's enormous family pitching in, the majority of the mess was gone in no time, the dog's fence had been rebuilt, and half a dozen grills sent delicious scents into the air.

They'd even helped run the marina while he dealt with everything else.

That drove it home for him: in Buckhorn, people helped each other. Gray liked that. A lot. It was so different from the city life he'd been used to, especially as a cop.

Petie, who'd worked as hard as anyone, wiped his hands on a towel and eyed Gray. "You're not going to let this run you off, are you?"

Gray laughed. "I was just thinking how glad I am that I moved here."

That pleased Petie. "Glad to hear it."

"Am I interrupting?" Lisa asked as she joined them.

"As if you could," Petie said. He scratched the graying beard stubble on his throat. "Guess I ought to get up to the store. It's lookin' busy." He went off and Shelby, no longer leashed, followed closely behind him.

Gray looked at Lisa. She looked…somehow distant as she stared after the dog.

Was she worried? Gray tipped her chin toward him. "Shelby is fine."

She bit her lip and stayed quiet.

More than once he'd heard her father and uncles expressing concern for her. Until their vandal was caught, her nearness to him could be dangerous.

Did she realize that, too? If so, it might make what he had to do easier—at least for her. "I'm sorry about all this." He put his arms around her and pulled her in. For most of the day she'd been inundated with family, all of them openly speculating. "You okay?"

Leaning back, she stared at him. "Me? I'm fine. I was worried about you."

*What the hell?* "I can take care of myself."

She laughed. "As can I."

"What? Take care of me?" He liked that idea.

Very seriously, she said, "If you ever need me, I'd be happy to help. But I meant that I can take care of myself, too."

He brought her in for a kiss. "And if you ever need me, for any reason, I'm here for you. You know that, right?" For him, that would never change, no matter how this all worked out.

Her smile went tender, her gaze searching. "So we can take care of ourselves, but we're each willing to care for the other, too?"

"You know what?" Amber said, interrupting the moment. "That sounds like a relationship to me."

With a theatrical groan, Lisa dropped her forehead to Gray's chest. "Why," she lamented, "does my family keep sneaking up on me today?"

"It only feels sneaky," Adam told her, "when you're hiding secrets."

"I'm not!" Lisa snapped, then tucked her face against Gray again.

Gray wisely stayed out of it.

"You are," Amber insisted, not worried about staying out of anything, apparently. "I just don't know why. I mean, we have eyes, you know. And look at him, Lisa. Most ladies would be bragging."

Gray grinned while stroking Lisa's back. "Thank you."

"You're welcome."

"I think it's because they barely know each other." Adam eyed him. "You really rushed things, didn't you?"

Lisa groaned, so Gray did more stroking along her spine. "She's irresistible. I couldn't help myself."

"Seriously?"

Amber shoved Adam. "Don't be a doofus. Uncle Sawyer met Honey and knew she was the one. And Dad met Mom and even though it took them a little longer to work things out, he knew she was special. And *your* dad," she continued, "met Georgia and flipped."

"Yeah," Adam said with a smile. "You're going off what you've been told, but even though I was young, I can still remember the first time Dad stayed over and made us pancakes."

Lisa shifted a little to see the others, but she stayed close. With a smile in her voice, she said, "He used a turkey baster to make the pancakes into shapes. Mom didn't know what to think of him. I remember her looking so confused."

Gray liked hearing the stories. It shored up his belief that sometimes you just knew when someone was the right one. For him, that someone was Lisa. For her... he just didn't know.

"You know," Amber said to Adam. "I have someone in mind for you, too, so if you—"

"What I want to know," Adam said, cutting her off, "is why all this trouble is following Gray."

Lisa pushed away from Gray to confront her brother. "It's not his fault that some idiot is into the destruction of property."

"Never said it was, but if it's the same idiot who wrote that note and damn near strangled a dog, then it has something to do with him, right?"

"He's being targeted!"

"But maybe by someone who knows him?"

Gray tried to interject, but he couldn't get a word in edgewise as the siblings squabbled back and forth. He looked at Amber, saw her smiling and shook his head.

She edged around Lisa and Adam and nudged him with her shoulder. "Usually Lisa is quiet."

"Ha!" Adam said.

"I am quiet!"

Gray grinned. "She's a delicate flower."

Sucking in air, Lisa rounded on him. "Are you saying I'm not?"

"I'm saying you're beautiful and smart and I enjoy you whether you're being pensive or giving your brother hell."

"Ooh," Amber said. "Not only gorgeous, but smooth."

Lisa narrowed her eyes at Amber, which only made Amber laugh. "Lighten up, cuz. If he's going to stick around—"

"He is," Gray confirmed.

"—then he may as well get used to us, right?"

"Not like any of you are giving him a choice."

"It's fine," Gray said. "Better than fine. I appreciate all the help today."

Looking closed off and distant, Lisa didn't reply.

Gray had no idea why she was so out of sorts. Well, except that someone had crept around the yard wreaking havoc while they slept. That could be unnerving her. But he sensed it was something more than that.

Something personal.

Maybe he should get her alone and find out.

He was about to suggest that when Amber hooked her arm through his. "So, Lisa, you're saying you don't have a claim in this one? Because if he's free, I know a few single ladies who would *love* for me to work my magic."

"No, thanks," Gray said hurriedly.

At the same time, Lisa growled, *"Don't even think it."*

"Yeah," Adam said, his tone dry. "Such a delicate flower."

Gray pulled Lisa back when she reached for her brother. "If you guys would excuse us a moment, I think Shelby needs us."

Since Shelby was sprawled under a big tree some distance away, sleeping soundly, it was an obvious lie.

Gray didn't care. Unfortunately, getting Lisa alone was like walking the gauntlet.

First he had to get past Morgan, Misty, Sawyer and Honey. The men looked at him with suspicion, but the women smiled their encouragement. Morgan's wife even gave him the thumbs-up.

Then they went around Gabe's daughters, who had effectively circled Tucker, not that Tucker seemed to mind all that much. Gabe didn't like it, though, and he was fast closing in on them, pausing only long enough to note Gray leading Lisa toward the house.

"Don't do anything I would do," he said to Gray, then pointed at his daughters. "That goes for you three, too."

The girls laughed, but Tucker held up his hands in a sign of innocence...while wearing a big grin.

Yeah, Gray wasn't buying that any more than Gabe did.

Jordan stood with Garrett and Shohn at one of the grills, and they all three stared as Gray, with his hand at Lisa's back, kept her walking.

"Should we save you some food?" Jordan asked mildly, and it looked like he was asking about a lot more than food.

"A burger each, please," Gray said, putting her father at ease. "We won't be long."

Jordan just nodded, but the two younger men snickered—and got threatened with a grill fork.

Inside the store provided no privacy, either, not with Petie now waiting on customers. Going upstairs to his living area would be too damn obvious, so Gray led Lisa right back out the front door, across the gravel lot and toward the large elm tree where Shelby slept on. She'd deliberately found a quiet spot away from the chaos. There were no benches here, only that one lone tree, a chicken-wire fence overgrown with weeds, and what felt like an army of bugs.

"Where," Lisa asked, "are we going?"

"Not sure yet," Gray told her. "So far the tree looks semiprivate, but with your family I'm never sure who might pop up next."

She groaned.

"I like them," Gray reminded her. He glanced back and saw a lot of people looking their way, but no one followed. Shelby slept on, so Gray kicked down the weeds in one spot, sat and pulled Lisa into his lap. "Now."

She tucked her face into his neck. "They do this sort of thing a lot."

Gray breathed in the scent of her sun-warmed hair and skin, and his body stirred. Nothing new in that. He pretty much wanted her around the clock. It was taking some time to get used to it and to get it under control. "What's that?"

Throwing out an arm, she indicated her family. "They circle the wagons, show up en masse to help out. They're...pretty wonderful."

"I agree." He nuzzled his way along her throat to her jaw, nudging her face up as he went so he could kiss her. "You think they like me okay?"

"They lo—"

His mouth over hers cut off her reply. As always, her soft lips opened to the touch of his tongue. Her breath hitched. She leaned into him, accepting. Participating.

And even here, with weeds poking him in the ass and a mosquito buzzing in his ear, with Shelby's snores and her family's whispers, he could so easily get lost in loving her.

But she was already shy about her family knowing how involved they were, so Gray forced himself to cool it. With one last stroke of his tongue over hers, he retreated, nibbled on her lips, then put his forehead to hers.

"I'm going to find whoever did this."

"Mmm-hmm." She tried to kiss him again.

"Hey." Gray let her take one quick kiss but didn't let it get too heated. "If we don't put the brakes on that, I won't be able to rejoin your family."

Sliding her arms around his neck, she hugged him. "You confuse me so much."

"Yeah?" The crook of her shoulder, her neck, smelled so good and felt so soft. "How's that, honey?" He stroked his hand up and down her back. No matter what Lisa wore, she always looked stylish and sexy but this, his shirt, thrown on hastily that morning when he'd called her for help, looked better on her than it ever could on him. She hadn't yet changed, so she also had on running shorts and bare feet, and he loved her. Her sleek runner's legs, her rounded ass, those cushiony breasts pressed to his chest. Her mouth. Her hugs and her sighs. Her strength and her humor, and her dedication to her family. Every inch of her, everything about her.

But he wouldn't manipulate her with words into doing anything that she didn't really want. So he kept his love to himself. "Lisa?" She'd gotten awfully quiet.

"You landed here after some pretty horrific circumstances, but now you just roll with it."

"It?"

"Everything. Anything." She shook her head. "Whatever happens."

Mostly because *she* had happened. With her, it didn't matter what else went wrong, it was still going to feel right.

Except that... Gray knew he couldn't take chances with her. He'd brought her here to find out what was on her mind, but realized he also needed to share what was on his.

"Your poor boat," she whispered and hugged him again as if she thought he might need the comfort.

"Yeah. Sucks. But it can be repaired." He brushed back her hair. "You can't."

"What?" She struggled to get free, but he held on.

"I'm going to get the loon who's targeting me. I swear I am. Tucker is on it, and so is your uncle, and everyone in your family is alert and keeping watch. But I don't feel right about you being here. Not until it's resolved."

She shoved back so hard she got away from him and, landing on her butt, bumped into Shelby. The dog jumped, looked at them both, then huffed and resettled herself.

"Are you all right?"

Eyes locked on his, she whispered, "You're ditching me."

"No! Never that." Gray reached for her but she dodged him. "If I could I'd move you in."

Her jaw loosened, then went tight. "You *could*," she said in a voice too high, then glanced at the crowd of her family and lowered her voice. "I've all but moved in on you anyway."

"Right." Bitterness leaking through, Gray said, "That's why you head home every morning so no one will know you spent the night."

She gasped, scowled and scampered closer to stick her face near his. "I was trying to be *considerate*."

"Considerate?" His own temper kicked in. "How the hell do you figure that?"

"You haven't asked me to stay, so I didn't push it. If my family once knew that we...that I..."

Glaring at her, he leaned in, too. "That we're committed to each other? I can say it even if you can't."

"I can say it!" But she faltered. "If it's true."

"Why the hell would you doubt it?"

"I doubt it because all you've done is explain to me how you're hunky-dory however it goes, if I stay, if I leave, oh, well, Gray will be fine."

He plopped back on his ass. "That's what you think?" God, he would *not* be fine if she ended things.

Her brows shot up. "That's what you've said."

"I was trying not to pressure you."

"Great," she snapped right back. "I'm not pressured."

At that moment, it almost struck him as funny, but he didn't dare laugh. Not with Lisa looking both hurt and mad. "I'm in love with you."

Her eyes went wide. *"What?"*

A whisper, not a shout. He smiled. "I love you. Hell, I've been in love with you since I saw you here again. Maybe even before that. Everything about you suits everything in me. I want you with me. I want you here in Buckhorn. But more than that, I want you happy. If your old job does it for you, then I'll—"

She landed against him, kissing his face, tumbling him backward onto the gravel-rough, weed-strewn, root-mangled ground. "Ow," he said and held her close.

"Oh, Gray," she breathed. "Crazy how it happened so fast, but you just said it so beautifully."

"What'd I say?" He couldn't think with her stretched out over him, her heart beating in time with his, a damned audience no doubt watching every move they made.

"Everything about you suits everything in me."

"Oh, right. That."

She laughed. "No, I was saying it to you."

Forgetting the audience, Gray grabbed her shoulders and lifted her. "You love me?"

Her beautiful, devastatingly dark eyes answered before she said, "Of course I do. You heard Amber." Her lips curled and she added with sassiness, "You're a catch."

He crushed her close, one hand in her hair, an arm across her back. His heart felt...explosive. As if it might punch right out of his chest. "I want you happy," he said again with conviction. He wanted that more than anything.

"I am."

Wanting to believe her, he asked, "Your career...?"

"I don't know, Gray." She kissed his throat, his chin, then nipped his bottom lip. "Somehow I'll work it out. But I don't want to give up you, *this*, just to chase a career I'm not sure I even want."

He searched her face and believed her. She wanted to stay. *With him.* As she'd said, they'd work out everything else. And thinking that, he sat up but kept her on his lap. "We need to talk."

"Gray," she warned.

"I have to know you're safe until I resolve the threat."

"A vandal isn't a threat."

"A vandal who leaves cowardly notes and abuses a stray dog is."

Her small hand settled against his jaw. "I'm not leaving you." She turned her head toward her gathered family members and said louder, "I don't care who knows about it."

Gray was more than ready to insist when Shelby came awake with a start, bolting to her feet, ears up, eyes alert.

Sniffing the air.

"What in the world?" Lisa said, already moving off his lap.

"Hey, girl." Gray stood and reached for the dog, but she stared off toward the weeds along the fence. Her lips curled in a snarl and, hunkering down, she began creeping forward.

Gray stared at the high weeds along the fence. "A critter, maybe?"

Shaken, Lisa shook her head. "I don't think so."

Suddenly Shelby lunged, filling the area with enraged barking as she ran. She went through a hole in the fence and Gray, running after her, went over the fence. He landed in prickly bushes and felt a scratch on his back, another on his leg. Behind him he heard Lisa yell and then the commotion as others followed.

Shelby launched herself and landed on a man holding a gas can. The can nearly dropped out of his hand, spilling everywhere as he attempted to protect himself.

In a matter of seconds Gray took it all in, and comprehension dawned. What looked like a very crude, makeshift bomb had been jammed up against the fence between a dead tree and a metal barrel full of debris, surrounded by dry brush. An oily path led to the man... and the spilled gas can.

The son of a bitch had planned a very big, loud fire.

*Dangerous.* Especially with so many people at the marina.

Enraged, Gray reached them, took Shelby's collar and hauled her back from the man's flailing fists and legs. Meaning it, he said, "Kick my dog, and I swear to God you'll regret it."

The man scampered back, breathing hard, his eyes a little wild. "Your dog attacked me!"

"Yeah." He kept his eyes on the man, but said, "Good dog."

Luckily, Shelby subsided, sitting down but still tense.

"Easy now." He stared down at the man—the same man who had thrown a kid in a lake, who had argued with Lisa and then been left ashore when his date took off with her son in the boat. Likely the same man who had tied that damned rope too tight around Shelby's neck. "I remember you."

The man kicked out at him, inciting Shelby all over again.

And then suddenly Morgan was there, saying, "Jordan's keeping Lisa back, and I've got the dog for you."

Satisfaction brought a smile to Gray's mouth. He didn't look back to confirm what Morgan said. He trusted him.

Releasing Shelby, he reached for the man.

Panicked, the idiot swung the gas can in an awkward arc. Gray ducked—and then drilled him. One clean shot to the chin that took the guy's feet out from under him. He went flat again, the can falling well out of his reach.

Suddenly Tucker snapped, "What the hell? Damn you, Morgan, why didn't you tell me?"

"You were busy flirting with Kady. Besides, I wanted to let Gray hit him a few times first."

Gray took advantage of that confession, hauling the man up and punching him one more time before Tucker bellowed, "That's enough!"

Knowing the procedure, Gray stepped back and began explaining everything while Tucker put the man in handcuffs.

Lisa joined him then, half her family following along. She stopped by Shelby, kneeling down to hug the dog. Shelby glanced at her, licked her face, then stared with evil intent at the man being led away.

Shohn and Garrett had just walked the fence. "The gas is all along the base of the fence," Shohn said. "Guess he planned a big fire."

"Guaranteeing he'd get away," Garrett said.

Still furious, Gray nodded. "It'd be hard to pursue him if we had to go through flames to do it."

Garrett surveyed everything, then rubbed the back of his neck. "I'm thinking you'll have to close the marina for a day so we can burn it off. Better that we do it before some kid gets more than he bargained for playing with matches."

"Agreed." Gray stared at Lisa. She hadn't yet come to him. "Lisa?"

She stayed by Shelby but looked up at him. With her cousins and uncles around her and other family crowding in, she said, "So I don't have to go back to my house."

Damn, but he loved her. He didn't look at anyone else, never broke eye contact with her. He just smiled. "No, you don't."

"This is one of those times," Morgan said, "when *not* being the cop is a good thing. Tucker will be tied up for hours with that ass, and you're free and clear."

"Yeah." Gray went to Lisa, pulled her up and against him and then kissed her silly.

He vaguely heard her brother say, "I feel like I should be protesting this."

"Do," Amber said, "and she'll annihilate you."

It wasn't until Shelby leaned against his leg that he managed to end the kiss. With one hand on Shelby's neck, the other at Lisa's waist, he said, "I love you."

She nodded, smiled. Blinked back a few tears. "I love you, too."

There was more murmuring about *fast*, but Gray ignored them all.

Shohn spoke up. "Does this mean you're staying?"

Gray was about to tell him not to pressure her, but Lisa said, "Yes!"

And then her family did so much cheering and carrying on that he couldn't get anything said. Men were shaking his hand, women were hugging him. He got separated from Lisa while the congrats went around.

He'd just gotten to her when Amber threw herself against him, squeezing him tight. For a slight woman, she had her fair share of strength.

Laughing, Gray accepted the hug until she dropped back to her feet. The second she freed him, he pulled Lisa close again.

"We're alone," Amber said to the two of them, "so I have a couple of things to say to you."

Lisa leaned into his side. "Beware, Gray. She has that intense look in her eyes that means she's about to shock us."

Amber started to speak but pulled back. "Do I really? I mean, I've heard that before. That I give myself away." Hands on her hips, more to herself than anyone else, she muttered, "Maybe that's why I can't catch Noel off guard."

"Noel?" Gray asked.

"Noel Poet," Lisa explained. "He's a firefighter with Garrett, and Amber's boyfriend."

Amber snorted. "He's never even kissed me, so how could he be my boyfriend?"

"My guess?" Gray smiled at her. "You probably scare the poor guy."

Amber looked thoughtful for a moment, then dismissed that notion with a shake of her head. "I don't scare you, right?"

"No." Because he'd only have peripheral involvement with her, through Lisa. But if he'd ever thought to get close to her, then hell, yes, she would scare him.

"There. I'm not scary at all."

"If I could make a suggestion?" Gray waited until he had the attention of both women. "If you want to kiss him, make a move. No reason you should have to wait."

"Hmm. You know, you could be right. If he was here today instead of on duty, I'd give it a shot just to see his reaction."

Gray grinned. Yeah, he believed her. Amber Hudson wouldn't shy away from many things—definitely not a man.

She shook her head. "So anyway, back to you guys. I was waiting, holding back until—"

He and Lisa both laughed.

"—I knew for sure you'd be working it out." She winked at Gray. "You haven't disappointed me. I don't even think you needed the incentive of the other guys I brought around to get you motivated."

Gray wasn't surprised to learn that had been her

ploy. "When it comes to Lisa, believe me, I'm very self-motivated."

"So I see."

"Amber," Lisa warned.

Amber leaned to look beyond them, around them, then she said, "High five, cuz."

Confused but compliant, Lisa smacked palms with Amber.

"Sometimes," Amber told her, "a one-night stand turns into forever. I'm proud of you! You went for it, so kudos to you."

Lisa went mute and Gray frowned. "How...?"

Waving a hand, Amber explained, "I knew where Lisa had traveled, and after grilling Gray when I first met him, I knew where he'd been. The timing lined up, so it seemed obvious to me, especially after seeing the two of you together. But don't worry. Your secret is safe with me."

Gray rubbed his face. Yeah, she was scary, all right.

"Now, about you staying in Buckhorn." Amber smiled at her red-faced cousin. "Have you thought about working remotely? Casey does it sometimes and he said all you'd really need is reliable internet, a quiet place to work, some meeting software and *voilà!* Cybermeetings, instead of face-to-face, are the in thing. You work out all the deets in online meetings, then limit your travel to a few days a month. What do you think?"

After a few expectant seconds when Lisa looked thunderstruck, she grabbed Amber, squealing as she hugged her.

Amber laughed with her. "So you like the idea?"

"I love the idea!" Lisa gave her cousin a big smooch,

then held her away. "I can't believe I didn't think of it. I mean, I've been involved in cybermeetings for different clients. I've just been so stressed, and then Gray was here, and..." Winding down, she said, "You're a genius."

"That's what I keep telling people." She held up her hand and Gray high-fived her as well. "My work here is done. Oh, how I love a happy ending." Clearly pleased with herself, Amber moseyed off.

Gray brought Lisa around for a quick kiss. "You think that would actually work?"

"As Amber said, it's the in thing. My company wants me, so I think they'll be all over it."

He searched her face and had to ask, "It'll make you happy?"

"You make me happy. Shelby makes me happy." She inched closer. "Keeping my job but losing all the travel will make me happy."

He grinned. "Then I'm happy, too." He touched her face. "And since you're compromising, what do you think about me doing the same?"

"How?"

"I'm not rushing you, I promise. But I want to marry you, and when we do—"

*"Gray."* She threw herself against him, bounced a little, then grabbed his face and kissed him.

Gray didn't mind the interruption, not with Lisa holding him tight, bubbling with excitement. But as the kiss ended, he grinned and asked, "Is that a yes?"

"Yes!"

Happiness threatened to take out his knees, but he stiffened his legs and kept her close to his heart. "We won't need two houses. Doesn't matter to me where we live, so either I'll rent out my house and Shelby and I will live with you, or you can sell your place and live here with us. I know it's small, but I thought it was just going to be me. Now that it's us, you and me and Shelby, we can remodel or add on."

She covered her mouth.

Gray hurried to say, "Or we can keep both and worry about it later. Or buy something new. Or build, or—"

*"Gray."* She said his name this time with tears in her eyes and a trembling smile. "Yes to marrying you, yes to having only one house for you and me and Shelby, but I honestly don't care which one." She inhaled, brushed a tear from her cheek. "Yes to loving you."

"And yes to staying in Buckhorn?"

"It's my home," she whispered. "I've always enjoyed it, but now that you're here, I never want to leave."

Together, they turned to head back to the gathering of her family. Lisa spotted Amber saying something to Adam while Adam tried to shake his head and refuse.

Lisa grinned. "It looks like my brother might be next on Amber's radar."

"Good. He's a nice guy. He should be happy." When Lisa slanted a dubious look up at him, Gray said, "What? She does good work. I trust she'll do right by him."

Lisa laughed over that, but she didn't deny it. Amber had been helpful, not that either of them had really needed a nudge.

Mingling into the crowd of Lisa's big family, with her at his side, Gray recognized the truth. He'd left behind his old life and all the strife. He'd have been happy with the slower lifestyle, the change of pace.

Instead, he'd gotten so much more.

Because now, he had it all.

* * * * *

*Keep reading for an excerpt from*
*DON'T TEMPT ME by Lori Foster*

Honor Brown wasn't used to eating with three men. It astounded her how fast the pizza got devoured. But then, she'd pretty much inhaled her own slice, too. Working up a hunger through unpacking all her belongings, it seemed, overshadowed other concerns—like feeling self-conscious and knowing she was an intruder despite her new neighbors' efforts to put her at ease.

They all chatted easily, except for Jason who seemed introspective. He'd gone from staring to teasing, to warning, and now quiet.

At first she'd worried that she might have offended him. But how? Not by asking that he wear a shirt, because that was a request he'd ignored.

The man was still half naked.

And it couldn't have been from accepting his help unloading her furniture, because he was the one who'd bullied his way in and insisted on…being wonderful.

She rubbed at her temples. When she'd imagined neighbors, she'd never imagined any like these.

"You okay?" Jason's nephew Colt asked.

A fast smile, meant to reassure the teen, only amplified the headache. "Yes. Just a little tired."

"She works too much." Lexie shoulder-bumped her. "I've tried to get her to play a little, too, but she's the original party pooper."

Lexie, at least, seemed right at home. But then she always did. Confident, beautiful and fun—that described her best friend.

They were polar opposites.

As if she'd known the guys forever, Lexie had heckled Hogan, teased Colt and praised Jason. Repeatedly she put her head back and drew in deep breaths, closing her eyes as she did so. Honor understood that. It was like being in a park with the scents of freshly mowed lawn, earth, flowers and trees all around them. Jason's backyard was a half acre, same as hers. But while hers was nearly impassable with weeds, his was park perfect.

A gigantic elm kept them shaded, and with the help of an occasional gentle breeze, the summer day became more comfortable. Honor glanced around at the neatly mulched flower beds, the velvet green grass and the well-maintained outdoor furniture. His garage was spectacular, matching his house. Every so often she caught the faint scent of oil, gasoline and sawdust.

She also smelled sun-warmed, hard-working male. Not at all unpleasant.

"Where do you work?" Colt asked.

"She's a stylist," Lexie offered. With a nod at Jason, she said, "Honor could do all sorts of amazing things with your hair."

Honor choked on her last sip of Coke.

Unaffected, Jason ran a hand through the dark waves. "I have a barber, but don't make it there as often as I should."

"He's always working," Colt said. "He's usually out there in the garage before Dad and I even get out of bed."

"Good thing messy looks so sexy on him, then, huh?"

Colt laughed. "If you say so."

"I do." Lexie half turned to face the garage. "You guys have a lot of vehicles."

"The blue truck is mine," Colt told her. "Dad drives the motorcycle. Or when it rains, he takes the Escort. Uncle Jason has his own truck, the red newer one, and the gray SUV. The flatbed truck he uses for deliveries."

Wow, so many vehicles. Honor glanced over and saw that the two-story garage also housed a fishing boat on a trailer, and another, older truck parked front and center.

"Who drives that one?" Lexie asked.

With something close to hero-worship, Colt said, "Uncle Jason was hired to work on it."

"Hired?"

"Yeah, that's what he does. He fixes things. He's really good, too. All these old houses? They're always needing something repaired and usually Uncle Jason can do it. Everyone around Clearbrook hires him for stuff."

"Sounds like it keeps him busy."

Colt snorted. "Yeah, sometimes too busy."

"I don't mind." Jason's gaze cut to Honor and his voice deepened. "I enjoy working with my hands."

Honor felt like he'd just stroked her. She caught her breath, shifted in her seat and tried to think of something to say.

Clearly tickled, Lexie looked back and forth between them. "So you're a handyman?"

Again, Colt bragged. "More like a contractor. He can build things from the ground up, including the plumbing and electrical. Or make stuff like custom gates or unique shutters, or repair just about anything."

"Nice," Lexie praised.

"He's a jack-of-all-trades." Hogan toasted Jason with his Coke. "Whatever's broke, Jason can fix it."

Jason gave him a long look. "Maybe not everything."

"Right. Can't fix big brothers, can you?"

Tipping his head slightly back, as if he'd taken that on the chin, Jason replied, "I only have one older brother, and far as I'm concerned, he's not broken."

Colt went silent, and God, Honor felt for him. Too many times she, too, had been caught up in the middle of squabbles.

"So with the truck," Lexie said, interrupting the heavy tension, "are you doing engine or body work?"

Before Jason could answer, Hogan said, "Why are you so curious, anyway?"

Lexie leveled him with a direct stare. "I was making conversation."

With a sound halfway between a laugh and a groan, Hogan sat forward. "We already covered that he can do anything."

"Anything is a big word. I mean, can he get the stick out of your butt? Because seriously, you're being a pill."

"He does both," Colt cut in, clearly anxious to keep things friendly. "Uncle Jason I mean. You asked about the truck?"

Lexie gave Colt a genuine smile. "So I did."

"He does body and engine work. But this time Uncle Jason's just tricking it out some."

Honor watched the back and forth conversation, noting the indulgent way Jason looked at his nephew, while also feeling the growing tension from Hogan. But why?

The quiet smothered her, especially with the palpable acrimony now flowing between Hogan and Lexie. After clearing her throat, Honor asked, "Is that what we interrupted when we first got here? You were working on the truck?"

Jason shook his head. "Tractor." He nodded toward the side of the garage. "The owner of the truck is making up his mind between two options I gave him. Today I was repairing the tractor, but it needs a part I won't have until tomorrow. I'm at a standstill on both projects so you didn't really interrupt. I was already done for the day."

Hogan ran a hand over his face, popped his neck and finally worked up a smile. "He built the garage a few years back."

"You helped," Jason reminded him.

"By *help*, he means I followed directions. No idea where Jason got the knack because our dad wasn't the handy sort. But if there's an upside to us staying with him right now, it's that he's teaching Colt."

"And Colt does appear to have the knack," Jason added.

Both Honor and Lexie looked at the garage with new eyes. Wow. Just...wow.

"It's unlike any garage I've ever seen."

"You should see the shed he did for Sullivan," Colt bragged. "And the gazebo for Nathan."

"Sullivan and Nathan?" Lexie perked up with interest.

"Other neighbors," Honor said before Lexie could

get started. She pushed to her feet while saying, "This was really wonderful. Thank you again, all of you."

When she started to pick up their paper plates, Colt took over. "I got it."

Unbelievable. She'd never known such a polite young man. "Are you sure?"

He grinned, looking like a younger version of his uncle. "Positive. It all just goes to the can." He gathered up everything and walked off.

Honor turned to Hogan. "You did an amazing job with him."

"Thanks. He's always been an easy kid. Smart, friendly and self-motivated."

Again, Honor wondered about Colt's mother. Had she taken a hand in molding such an impressive young man?

Hogan said, "I need to take off now, too."

"Big date?" The way Lexie asked that, it was clear to one and all she didn't expect it to be.

"Actually," Hogan said, "yes."

In an effort to stem new hostilities, Honor stepped in front of her friend. "I hope we didn't hold you up."

"Nope. I have a few minutes yet." His frown moved past Honor to Lexie. "Guess I need to go change, though."

Laughing, Lexie asked, "Need fashion advice?"

His dark expression softened. "I think I've got it covered."

She nodded while yawning. "I need to get going, too."

"Gotta catch up on your beauty sleep?"

Honor almost groaned...until Lexie laughed again.

"Good one," she said, and then she held up her

palm, leaving Hogan no choice but to high-five her. To Jason, she teased, "The differences aren't just in looks, I take it."

Jason lifted a brow. "No, they aren't."

Without comment, Hogan headed off for the house.

"Well." Honor watched everyone depart. Hogan went into the house from the back door. Lexie headed off to the rental truck. And Colt hadn't returned from taking away their trash.

She and Jason were alone and with every fiber of her being, she felt it. Hoping not to be too obvious, she took a step back, then another. "I should get going, too. I need to drop off the truck tonight so I can get my car back. After I run Lexie home, I need to stop at the grocery. It's going to take me a few hours to get back here, and I still have to get things set up for the morning."

"What kind of things?"

"Alarm clock, coffee, and I have to unpack enough clothes to get ready for work in the morning."

He had been looking down at the ground as they walked, but now his head lifted and he stared at her. "You have to work tomorrow?"

"Yes." But it wasn't a matter of having to. "I'll be taking all the hours I can get for a while. There are so many things I want to do to the house, but it all takes funds." Funds she didn't have. What money she'd saved would go to dire necessities, so overtime helped to pay for the extras she wanted.

"You have to be tired."

"A little." She rolled her aching shoulders, but resisted the long stretch. "I'm both excited and exhausted and I don't know if I'd be able to sleep anyway."

"Excited?"

There were a hundred different reasons for her excitement and one of those reasons was standing before her. Jason Guthrie was about the sexiest man she'd ever met. His careless hair, strong features, dark eyes and that body... Yup. The body definitely factored in.

But she also liked his intense focus, the way he smiled with pleasure at his nephew, and his up-front honesty. That honesty had stung a little, since he clearly felt she was out of her league. Then again, he'd pitched in and done what he could to make her move-in easier.

How could she not admire him?

Naturally she wouldn't say any of that to him, so instead she shared other thoughts. "The move, the house—now that it's officially mine and I'm here, there are a million things running through my mind. What to do first, how much money I'll need, how to do it and when to do it." She smiled up at him. "Tonight, I might just dance around and enjoy it all."

"Yeah? Well, since you don't have curtains yet, I might watch."

She laughed at his teasing. "After I get the windows covered, then I'll dance."

His smile warmed. "Spoilsport."

Their shoulders bumped, electrifying Honor. She took a step to the side, ensuring it wouldn't happen again.

"I get it," Jason told her. "First big night in your own place." Lifting a brow, he added, "And yeah, curtains might not be a bad idea. Or at least tack up a sheet or something."

Maybe, Honor thought, he didn't dislike her as a neighbor as much as she'd assumed.

Stopping in the side yard, well out of range of everyone else, Honor looked up at him. Way up because he was so much taller than her.

He stopped, too, his expression attentive.

She shouldn't ask, but she had to. "When we first met...when I hit your trash can?"

"I told you, no big deal."

"I know, but...is that why you kept staring at me?"

Those gorgeous dark eyes caressed her face. He glanced toward Colt, then over to watch Lexie climb into the passenger seat of the truck.

Finally his gaze came back to hers, and the impact took her breath.

"For one thing," he said in a low voice, "you're attractive."

Without thinking about it, Honor smoothed her ponytail and tucked a few loose tendrils behind her ears. "Um, thank you. But I'm such a mess today."

His gaze warmed even more. "Messy and a mess are two very different things."

That deep voice made her pulse race. She was such an inexperienced dweeb, she wasn't sure how to respond, so she just nodded and said, "Okay."

A fleeting smile teased his mouth before he grew somber. "I also recognize trouble when I see it."

She tucked in her chin. "Trouble?"

"You."

"Me?" The question emerged as a squeak.

"You don't fit the mold, Honor Brown. Not even close."

A rush of umbrage helped to steady her voice. "What's that supposed to mean?"

"A certain type of person moves here. Not just to the area, but to this particular block. Mostly single men who can handle themselves. Men with some contractor skills, with time and ability to do the repairs needed. Young women—"

"I'm twenty-nine!"

"—who are completely alone do not set up house here."

It hurt to know he was right, that she was alone. She had Lexie, but it wasn't the same as a significant other or family who cared. She huffed, then deflated. "Well, this sucks."

He hesitated, but finally asked, "What does?"

Putting her nose in the air, Honor stared into his beautiful brown eyes. "I haven't even finished moving in, and already I dislike my neighbor."

On that parting remark, she turned and strode away. But her heart was thumping and her hands felt clammy and her stomach hurt.

She was never that rude. *What in the world got into me?*

Right before she reached the truck she glanced over her shoulder and saw Jason still standing there, hands on his hips, that laser-like gaze boring into her.

Damn it. She turned to fully face him. "Jason?"

His chin notched up in query.

"I apologize. I didn't mean it." Immediately she felt better—even with Lexie now laughing at her.

Jason's hands fell to his sides and he dropped his head forward. She saw his shoulders moving.

Laughing? She wasn't sure.

But she smiled and started to turn away again.

"Honor."

She peeked at him and found his hands were back on his hips.

"You're still trouble, no doubt about it. But if you need anything, let me know."

Sure. When hell froze over. She smiled sweetly, waved and finally got in the truck.

Copyright © 2016 by Lori Foster